Harvest
of Love

First edition, GreenWords Media, 2018

Harvest

of Love

— an Arcadia Valley Romance —

VALERIE COMER

GreenWords Media

Acknowledgments

I'm so thankful for my fellow Arcadia Valley Romance authors: Mary Jane Hathaway, Elizabeth Maddrey, Lee Tobin McClain, Danica Favorite, and Annalisa Daughety. If you haven't been following the multi-author series thus far, you really need to jump in and check out all the books at ArcadiaValley Romance.com! You'll find the characters behind Delis sausages, A Slice of Heaven bakery, El Corazon, Bigby Farm, and the Arcadia Valley Farmers Market, and if you read *their* books, you'll find references to my characters as well! Start with *Romance Grows in Arcadia Valley*.

Brainstorming with Elizabeth Maddrey always sparks fun new ideas for my stories. This time it was she who came to me in the fall of 2017, wondering what I thought about her next hero, Jonah Baxter, dating my next heroine, Kenia Akers, for a bit at the beginning of her novel *Donuts & Daydreams*. We tossed scenarios back and forth and decided this situation could provide a perfect backdrop to both of our upcoming novels.

I can't say enough good things about my editor, Nicole, who's been with me since before the beginning of my publishing career. Her keen eye and apt comments are so appreciated, as is her precious friendship.

Thanks to my husband, Jim, who chauffeured me on a road trip to the Twin Falls, Idaho, area in October, 2016, waited patiently while I took nearly a thousand reference photos, and offered his insights of our experiences. I love you, sweetheart. It's you who keeps my love for romance alive.

My husband is also the inspiration for Zane's struggles with Scotopic Sensitivity Syndrome, also known as Irlen Syndrome. Jim's struggles were not nearly as severe as Zane's — thank the Lord for that! — but his experiences and the research we did in 2007 with his diagnosis became the framework for Zane's history. SSS/IS is a real thing, and so is the solution, even though it sounds hokey as several characters in *Harvest of Love* mentioned!

Thanks to my kids, their spouses, and my grandgirls for their support and interest in my many projects. Special thanks to my daughter who's the cover designer for the entire Arcadia Valley Romance series. It's been fun sharing her expertise with my fellow authors.

I'm always thankful for my fellow inspirational romance author friends at Inspy Romance and my Christian Indie Authors group. I appreciate all who walk the journey with me both personally and professionally.

Thanks to my many readers and fans who've made their home in Arcadia Valley

"It is for this reason that I bow my knees before the Father, after whom all families in heaven above and on earth below receive their names, and pray:

"Father, out of Your honorable and glorious riches, strengthen Your people. Fill their souls with the power of Your Spirit so that through faith the Anointed One will reside in their hearts. **May love be the rich soil where their lives take root.** May it be the bedrock where their lives are founded so that together with all of Your people they will have the power to understand that the love of the Anointed is infinitely long, wide, high, and deep, surpassing everything anyone previously experienced. God, may Your fullness flood their entire beings." (Ephesians 3:14-19 The Voice)

Thank You, Jesus, my Redeemer.

Books by Valerie Comer

Arcadia Valley Romance Novels

Romance Grows in Arcadia Valley
Sprouts of Love
Rooted in Love
Harvest of Love

Farm Fresh Romance Novels

Raspberries and Vinegar
Wild Mint Tea
Sweetened with Honey
Dandelions for Dinner
Plum Upside Down
Berry on Top

Riverbend Romance Novellas

Secretly Yours
Pinky Promise
Sweet Serenade
Team Bride
Merry Kisses

Urban Farm Fresh Romance Novels

Promise of Peppermint
Secrets of Sunbeams
Butterflies on Breezes
Memories of Mist
Wishes on Wildflowers

Christmas in Montana Romances

More Than a Tiara
Other Than a Halo
Better Than a Crown

Chapter 1

KENIA AKERS SHIFTED from one foot to the other at the back of the huge Bigby barn. She shouldn't have come to the benefit concert, but it had seemed even more depressing to stay home on Valentine's Day when she'd been planning to attend for weeks. She'd dumped Jonah yesterday, but that was no reason to let her ticket go to waste. Maybe he'd use his for a bookmark... if he even had time to read since he was obviously pursuing Gloria Sinclair again. Jerk.

Wasn't it just Kenia's luck? Meet an adorable guy like Jonah Baxter on Christmas Eve, be wooed with whirlwind dates, only to discover he was still in love with someone else on February thirteenth?

She should've waited until after the concert to send him packing. At least she would have had one perfect Valentine's Day to remember. She'd have been here on the arm of one of the cutest, sweetest men she'd ever met instead of solo with half the town wondering about the demise of her short romance.

Kenia choked back a snort and tipped her chin up. Right. A perfect Valentine's Day, knowing he loved someone else?

On stage, Cole Anderson stood alone in the spotlight with his guitar as the elderly granny who'd sung the last song with him made her way down the steps and into the hushed audience. The spotlight divided, part of it coming to rest on Allie Bigby, the beneficiary of tonight's concert and silent auction. It sure stunk that Allie's lavender barn had burned down early Christmas morning. Then there'd been some glitch with her insurance. Arcadia Valley had pulled together to help raise the funds for rebuilding.

The mood shifted in the barn in that one long moment as Cole gazed down at Allie and Allie gazed back, her lips slightly parted and her eyes shining.

No way. There was only one thing that could be coming next, and it wasn't something Kenia wanted to witness. She pivoted for the door, only to discover she was blocked in by a wall of bodies. "Excuse me, please," she whispered once, twice, ten times as she edged toward the cold wintry night.

Cole's voice pushed into Kenia's consciousness. "Allie told me she loved me today, and I think you all know I love her, too."

Freedom beckoned from two people away. Kenia ducked between them, but one shifted and she connected with a hard elbow to her shoulder, spinning her sideways.

A warm hand caught her arm, steadying her, as startled eyes swung to meet hers. "I'm sorry. I didn't see you there."

Kenia stared into the gorgeous eyes of the man a few inches from her and tried to remember her words. His brown hair in need of a cut and his scruffy chin in need of a shave gave him a bad-boy image, unlike Jonah, Mr. Perfect.

On stage, Cole began singing a love song.

Immeasurably better than a proposal, but no doubt one was coming. This song was only a reprieve but, knowing Cole and Allie's history, he'd had years — decades — of unrequited love to pen at least twenty-five stanzas.

That didn't mean she should stand here like she'd been struck by lightning staring at a total stranger until Cole's final strum.

"Excuse me, please." Too bad she couldn't muster anything other than a breathless whisper.

A grin crinkled his face and warmed those eyes just as the heat of his hand left her arm.

Kenia yanked her gaze away and pushed open the barn door. Outside, icy air chilled her heated cheeks as she dashed across the crowded parking area to her car. A motion sensor blinked a light into action, cutting the view of the smattering of stars that bravely attempted illumination of the dark night.

With shaking hands, Kenia stuffed the key in her ignition, started her Ford Fiesta, and drove away from Bigby Farm. Whew. At least she'd missed the proposal. Sure, she was happy for Allie. She'd known the woman since high school. If anyone deserved to find true love and happiness, it was Allie.

Only... why not Kenia? Why had she wasted six weeks dating a man who couldn't stop dreaming about another woman? There'd been niggles of doubt, but she'd ignored them. She'd known Jonah'd had a thing for Gloria Sinclair for several years, but it had never gone anywhere. Kenia hadn't thrown herself at him. He'd been the one to invite her to his brother's wedding. He'd been the one to hold her close while they danced, who'd kissed her, albeit briefly, at the stroke of midnight on New Year's. He'd been the one who'd invited her to his family dinners, cooked her amazing meals, and snuggled her while they watched movies.

She hadn't dreamed all that. He'd been the one pursuing her. Hadn't he?

Okay, maybe his kisses had lacked passion, but that had been welcome after Damian who'd groped her on their first and only date. Passion would build as their relationship developed and, one day, he'd ask her to marry him. She'd become Kenia Baxter. There'd be total fireworks by then.

Or not. She should've seen it coming. Should have, but hadn't. Not until yesterday when Gloria entered A Slice of Heaven, the bakery run by the Baxter family, and caught Kenia kissing Jonah. He'd been distracted. He'd made donuts for Gloria — expected her — and Kenia could tell he hoped she hadn't figured that out. He'd called Gloria when his sister had been rushed to the hospital to save the life of her unborn baby. Not Kenia. No, *she* found out accidentally, after the fact.

Having those blinders ripped off had been painful, but she had to hold her head up high in the community. Arcadia Valley was small, and everyone knew everyone else's business. Kenia managed Page Turners, her aunt's bookstore, so escaping town wasn't an option. The only salve she'd been able to muster had been breaking up with Jonah before he broke up with her.

She'd brought the basket of books and the Page Turners gift certificate out to the benefit concert as promised, ready to tell anyone who noticed she was alone that she'd called it off with Jonah. She hadn't expected to be required to witness Cole Anderson proposing to Allie Bigby.

That guy in the back of the barn. Who was he? Not a reader, or she'd have seen him in the bookstore...

unless he was one of those who preferred e-books or bought his paperbacks online. She shuddered. Maybe he was a friend of Cole's from out of town, just visiting for the concert. Probably that was it. A better thought than him not being a reader or not supporting the local bookstore.

Kenia pulled into the parking spot in front of her small cottage. She'd never see him again. That was fine. She needed time for her broken heart to mend.

The guy on the stage crooned on and on, obviously besotted with the young woman in the other spotlight. She was kind of pretty, with her tousled brown hair falling to her shoulders, but not as pretty as the woman he'd elbowed as she dodged past.

Zane Russell glanced at his friend Quinn standing beside him. "Who was that?"

"The girl who left in such a hurry? Kenia Akers. Wonder what her problem was." Quinn shrugged. "She runs the bookstore downtown."

Bookstore. Zane should forget about her right this minute. Forget about her short but fiery orange hair, forget about the sadness in her eyes... had they been blue? Hard to tell in the dim light. "Married?" Man, had that really come out?

Quinn's eyebrows pulled together as he gave Zane

his full attention for a minute. "Who are you talking about? Kenia? No, she's not married. I think she's dating someone, though. Last I heard, not that I keep track."

"It's Valentine's Day. If she were dating, she wouldn't have been sad and alone."

"So maybe they broke up." Quinn shrugged and faced the front, where the final guitar strums finally faded.

There was a silent auction spread out on tables across the back of the barn. Surely a local bookstore would have donated something to such a worthy cause. Zane wended his way through the standing guests, vaguely aware of the musician asking the woman to marry him. By the cheering of the crowd, she said yes.

Ah, there was a stack of books wrapped together with a band of brown paper on the back table. He didn't bother scanning the titles, just glanced at the bid sheet. Someone had bid $100. They were hardcovers. Probably worth that much or more on eBay. He scrawled $125 below it. Beside it was a listing for a $75 gift certificate with the same emblem as the paper by the books. The last bid was $80. He scribbled $100 on that one. Hopefully the engagement would keep people from coming to the back table to check their bids.

Wait, this was a stupid idea. He didn't need to spend money to find her store and introduce himself. Almost all the businesses in town were along Main Street or in that mini-mall where the bakery was. He could just stroll down the sidewalk and find the bookstore easily enough.

Russell, you're an idiot. You don't even read.

Yeah, well. Maybe he'd start.

The voice in his head burst out laughing. Okay, fine. It was unlikely. Anyway, Kenia Akers probably had other hobbies. She was around books all day at work, so she likely did other things in the evenings. Hiking, maybe. Biking. Kayaking. Of course, it was well below zero outside in mid-February, so he'd need other ideas to tide him through until warmer weather. He'd think of something.

A guy about Zane's age moved to the table closest to the door and tapped a wireless microphone. "Can I get everyone's attention, please? I'm Andrew Bigby, and I'd like to thank everyone for coming tonight and helping my sister's lavender business get back off the ground. Your generosity means a lot to our whole family. The silent auction has wrapped up, so let me just announce the lucky winners. If your name is called, please make your way to the item you bid on, and my wife, Layla, will accept your payment. Okay? Let's get going then."

Panic seized Zane's throat. Had he really bid on both the bookstore packages? And no one else was hurrying over to up the bid? *Come on, somebody.* His eyes scanned the crowd, but they all seemed content with whatever the outcome would be.

"The final bid on a bouquet from Blossoms by the Akers is one hundred eighty dollars. The bidder is Emerson Hadley. Thank you, Emerson and Blossoms by the Akers."

Andrew shifted to the next item. "The final bid on a three-day rafting trip is nine hundred fifty dollars. Thank you, Felipe Espinoza, for that great bid on a package by Snake River Tours."

A Latino man jogged to the back, pumping his fists, as a few people cheered.

"Well, that ought to be interesting," murmured Quinn from beside Zane. "He's a cop with five kids, all girls."

Zane tried for a chuckle, but it was hard.

Andrew picked up the next sheet. "The final bid on a seventy-five dollar gift certificate to Page Turners is one hundred dollars." He squinted at the paper. "Thank you, Zane Russell and to Page Turners for your donation. Wait, the next one is also from Page Turners for a set of six romance novels. Zane Russell, you're also the high bidder on this package with a bid of one hundred twenty-five dollars. Thank you."

An elbow caught the middle of Zane's back. "You bought a set of trashy romance novels?" Quinn chortled. "What were you thinking, man?"

Heat crept up Zane's cheeks. He should've taken a

closer look. The bid sheet had been on top, but he hadn't even looked at the covers. He'd only been thinking about a chance to meet Kenia Akers. Well, he'd get that chance, times two. Although the books were right here, and once he'd paid for them, he'd take them home. No trip to a bookstore would be necessary. What an idiot.

With wooden legs he moved over to where Layla was accepting a check from the police officer. Hopefully she had a method of accepting charge cards, too. He hadn't exactly intended to spend anything tonight.

She shifted her attention to him with a bright smile. "Your name?"

"Uh. Zane. Zane Russell."

Layla grinned. "That will be two hundred twenty five dollars, Mr. Russell. You must be an avid reader."

Best not to answer that part. He pulled out his wallet. "Can you take Visa?"

"Sure." She pulled out a cell phone and attached a small device. "I'll slide your card right through here."

"Great." He waited for the transaction to be complete then tucked the gift certificate into his wallet along with the card. Hopefully the bookstore also stocked gift items. Didn't most of them?

Then he reached for the stack of books. Man, he couldn't believe he'd let temporary insanity rule.

"Oh, wow, I was counting on winning that bid." A young woman dragging a small child by the hand glanced at the books and shook her head with a smile. "The one on top just came in this week, hot off the press, but I hadn't made it down to Page Turners to buy a copy yet. I've been waiting to get into this series until all the books were out."

Zane thrust the pile toward her. "Here you go."

"What?" Her startled eyes met his. "No. You bought them."

"That's okay. Really. You can have them. Happy Valentine's Day or something." Romance novels for Valentine's. Sounded like a match made in heaven.

Her gaze lingered on the books then shifted back to him. "Are you sure? I'm happy to pay you for them."

"Absolutely certain. Enjoy."

"But your wife... or girlfriend..."

"I think she's probably read them, after all." It was only a little white lie. If he had a girlfriend like Kenia — crazy thought that had possessed him — she would have read them by now, right?

Zane pushed the stack at the woman until her hands came up to accept the books. Then he nodded abruptly and edged his way out of the hot, crowded barn into the chilly parking area.

He should've come out here first, before doing something so stupid as bidding on a stack of books. If he'd thought at all, which he hadn't, he'd have assumed they were mysteries or maybe science fiction. Thrillers, maybe. But romance novels?

If he were a reader, he would've kept them. Maybe found some ideas on how to win a woman over. But, yeah, he wasn't a reader.

Chapter 2

*K*ENIA SIGNED FOR THREE BOXES of freight and handed the electronic device back to the UPS delivery woman. "Thanks so much. I've been waiting for these."

Perlita Ricci grinned at her. "Glad to oblige. I've been waiting, too. Do you suppose that whodunnit I ordered is in there?"

"Oh? I didn't see an order with your name on it. Irene must have been in that day." Not a big surprise. A lot of the older clients preferred to deal with Kenia's aunt, who'd opened Page Turners thirty years back after the death of her husband.

Kenia opened the drawer and reached for the box cutter. "What title was it?"

Perlita offered the information as she eyed the box, leaning against the counter.

After removing a wad of crumpled brown paper, Kenia began stacking paperbacks on the counter beside the cash register. "Oh, here's the one. Do you want it right now? I need to enter it into inventory before I can sell it, but that doesn't take long."

The other woman rubbed her hands together. "Yes, please. I can wait a few minutes."

The bells over the door jingled as another customer entered the bookstore, accompanied by a blast of cold winter air. Kenia glanced up, and her fingers froze around the mystery in her hand. Wasn't that the guy from the barn the other night? She'd only caught a glimpse of him, really, but the unruly brown hair and striking eyes were fixed in her memory. It had to be him.

The man stood just inside the door, shifting from one hiking boot to the other, as he glanced around. His nostrils flared slightly, and then his eyes found hers and seemed to cling.

Whoa. Definitely the same guy, but instead of her being the one running away this time, it looked like he was ready to bolt any second.

She took a deep breath. "Hi. Can I help you?"

His gaze jerked to the delivery woman then back to her. "I can come back some other time." He reached behind him for the door handle.

Odd reaction. Kenia frowned. "I'll only be a minute. Feel free to browse while I ring up this customer. We have a good selection in every genre and, if we don't have the one you're looking for, I can get it in just a few days."

Perlita nodded. "The service at Page Turners is really fast, just about as quick as ordering online. You can't go wrong."

"I, uh..." He shook himself visibly. "Okay. I can take a minute."

Kenia entered the title in her hand into inventory then rang up the sale. She kept an eye on the guy while Perlita swiped her card. Strange. He didn't take a single step toward the stacks. If anything, his wary gaze made her wonder what he was seeing that she didn't. Or was he, possibly, up to no good?

Perlita clutched the book to her chest dramatically. "Thanks so much. If this story is half as good as I expect it to be, I'll recommend it to my book club and order the rest of the series."

The perfect customer. Kenia smiled at her warmly. "Let me know. I haven't read that author yet."

"You read mysteries?"

"Sure do. I read everything. Well, except for horror, though we do stock some. I like sleeping at night, not freaking out over what's going to attack from the darkness." Maybe the guy had read too much horror and his imagination was in overdrive.

"This is just enough suspense for me." Perlita hugged her book and turned to the door. "Gotta run. Thank you!"

The man shifted out of the way as the delivery woman bustled out the door then jumped into her brown van with a wave.

Kenia came around the counter. "What can I help you find?"

He took a deep breath. "I'm Zane Russell."

When he didn't continue, she held out her hand. "Pleased to meet you. I'm Kenia Akers."

"I know." A flush threaded its way up through the stubble on his cheeks. "I mean, it's my pleasure to meet you."

She grinned. Sure, that's what he meant.

He reached into the pocket of his black jacket and pulled out a wad of paper. When he'd unfolded it, she recognized a Page Turners gift certificate.

"Oh! You were the high bidder at the silent auction?" Maybe he wasn't a serial killer after all.

Zane nodded and flicked a glance at her. "I thought you might have something besides books."

She raised her eyebrows at him. "It's a bookstore." She pointed at the logo on the paper with its open book and fluttering pages then spread her hands to indicate the entire space.

"Yeah, I see that." He shifted to his other foot and took a deep breath. "Man, I'm botching this. I saw you at the auction, and I wanted to introduce myself. I didn't think it would be this hard."

Kenia's gut fluttered. He'd felt the connection in that

brief instant, too? She rested her hand on his arm. "I'm glad you came in."

He froze, staring down at her fingers.

What, did she have a hangnail? Her orange gel nails looked fine to her. Maybe it was the peridot birthstone ring that had snagged his attention. Did he think it might be an engagement or promise ring even though on her right hand? There *was* a circle of small diamonds surrounding the stone. She wiggled her fingers. "Like my ring? My parents gave it to me for my eighteenth birthday."

Zane glanced up, the wariness seeping away. "It's cool. I haven't seen one like it before."

"I love it. That shade of green is such a cheerful color. I'm thankful to have been born in August and have a gorgeous birthstone. What's yours?"

"I, uh, never really thought about it. I was born in November."

"Oh, that's the topaz. Such depth to the colors, all brown and gold." She stepped to a nearby spinner rack, plucked a book out, and flipped it open to show him the November page. "This shows all the birthstones and gives their history. Fascinating."

He shook his head slightly.

"But that's not why you came in." Kenia tucked the paperback into its slot. He'd come in looking for something that wasn't books. Lots of bigger bookstores had coffee shops and an array of games and gifts, but not Page Turners. The space wasn't big enough to widen the selection, and they had a reputation for being well-stocked. Perlita Ricci wasn't the only resident of nearby Twin Falls who preferred to shop here.

"I'm not much of a reader."

That definitely explained the deer-caught-in-the-headlights sheen on his face when he'd entered. She smiled at him. "You probably just haven't met the right author yet. What kind of movies do you like?"

His dark eyes looked deeply into hers.

Kenia inhaled sharply and backed up a step. She could drown in that intense gaze.

"I know this is kind of weird and you don't know me at all, but I was wondering if you'd like to go out with me. We could catch a movie or a concert, or just do dinner if you prefer. Whichever. No pressure."

A guy who didn't read? What would they even talk about? She'd spent long evenings with her head in Jonah's lap while they talked about stories they both loved... although that hadn't been enough to keep them together. How could she even think about dating a man who didn't read? And, how about spiritually? Jonah at least attended Grace Fellowship. She hadn't seen Zane in church. She'd remember him, no doubt. If she and Jonah, who'd been so compatible, couldn't make it work, there wasn't any hope for someone else. She just didn't have the heart to try to get to know another guy and allow her hopes to rise.

Kenia shook her head and turned away. "Sorry. I'm not dating right now." As of three days ago.

⁂

Zane stumbled out of the bookstore, still clutching the piece of paper. That had been a colossal waste of time, to say nothing of money. Two hundred twenty-five dollars. He'd given that stack of books to the eager woman at the silent auction, and now he couldn't even find something to spend the gift certificate on. Who knew they didn't sell anything but books?

Yeah, yeah. He should've figured. He'd gambled on trying to get a pretty woman's attention. He'd had it for all of five minutes — wow, those startling blue eyes — and then *bam*, she'd turned him down. Okay, she didn't know him from Adam, but how could they get to know each other without spending time together?

He was still grumpy when he let himself into the house he shared with Quinn Lawson and Tony Santoro. Both guys were out of the house a lot — Quinn working and playing hard with Snake River Tours, his outdoor adventure company, and Tony as a chef at Italiana, his uncle's restaurant in Twin Falls.

Tony looked up from his tablet lying on the kitchen table in front of him. "Hey, Russell. Don't you have to work today?"

Zane glanced at the tablet, covered with words.

Valerie Comer

News? A blog? An e-book? His housemate always seemed to be reading something. "Yeah, I'm heading in soon. I'm taking a group of residents swimming at the Y this afternoon, and then some guy with a guitar is coming into Retro Village to do a concert right after supper, so I shifted my hours a bit later today."

"Sounds fun." Tony looked at the clock and stretched. "I've got a couple of hours before I have to leave."

"I've been wondering. How did you decide you wanted to be a chef?" Zane couldn't imagine being the activities coordinator at Retro Village for the rest of his working life. It wasn't that exciting.

"I started as a dishwasher in a restaurant in Galena Landing when I was in high school." Tony chuckled. "Got myself fired for being too mouthy, but I still say my boss was a jerk."

Zane leaned against the end of the cupboard. "Doesn't sound like an auspicious beginning."

"The head chef took a contract cooking for a tree-planting crew for a couple of months, and she hired me. I worked my butt off after school and weekends and learned a lot from her. After graduation, I went to culinary school in Seattle." He shrugged. "The rest, as they say, is history."

Figured there'd be school involved. "Anyone ever just learn on the job?"

"Yeah, sometimes. It tends to limit your options,

though. I worked in a couple of high-end restaurants in Seattle that wouldn't have hired me without credentials. Uncle Leo would've, of course. I'm soaking up all the traditional Italian tricks and tips I can from him, because I figure on opening my own restaurant before I'm thirty."

Zane was staring thirty in the face and had no such aspirations. He shook his head. "Going to give your uncle's restaurant competition?"

"Nah. There's a big Italian community in Spokane. Most of my dad's side of the family is there. I figure it's a good spot. Big enough city but not too big, if you know what I mean."

"Makes sense." Zane had heard his housemate talk about his extended family before. Must be nice to have a lot of relatives, though it was probably a mixed blessing.

"You? Your job require a degree?"

Was this where he admitted to dropping out of school? Zane grimaced. "No. I mostly make it up as I go, balancing what the residents want with how much budget the management sets for activities." Numbers he could do. They weren't easy, but they were better than words, at least when they came in color-coded columns on a spreadsheet.

"Gives you a lot of variety in your job, though. That's a bonus." Tony poked some buttons then shoved his tablet toward Zane. "Here, I came across this article the other day about getting seniors involved in cooking. You might find something useful in it."

Zane picked up the device and studied it while the words rolled like waves on the ocean. "Hmm. Maybe email me the link? I'll give it a look later."

"Sure, man. I can do that." Tony's fingers flew over a keyboard that appeared like magic. "Sent."

"Great, thanks. Always looking for new ideas. Job security, you know."

Tony laughed. "I get it. There's some chicken parm in the fridge if you're hunting food before going to work."

"I'll never say no if you're cooking, Santoro. Trust me." Zane dug the container from the second shelf and stuck it in the microwave for two minutes before digging in. By then his housemate was deep in whatever he was reading again, his thumb rhythmically swiping every few seconds.

What must it be like to tame the words and make sense of them? Seemed like everyone else on the planet could do it effortlessly. Either that, or they faked it even better than he did. He could puzzle out the meaning if he tried hard enough, but the headache was rarely worth it, especially not since he'd figured out how to have his phone read things to him. That had been a game changer.

Zane stuck in his earbuds and cranked some music while he savored the chicken parmesan. What he wouldn't give to cook like this. Read recipes and know he could find his place again if he looked away to add an ingredient.

Would Tony teach him if he asked? He studied the top of his housemate's dark head, bent over his tablet. Probably not. Tony could teach the cooking part, but even he couldn't make the words stay put. No one could. There wasn't any point in admitting his problem out loud when no one could solve it. Not him, not anyone else.

Chapter 3

KENIA TAPPED THE ENTRY CODE onto the door of the Frank Sinatra Pod in Retro Village. When it swung open, she scanned the common room for Granddad, but he wasn't sitting at the jigsaw puzzle table with his usual cronies. He wasn't among those gathered around Blake Taylor and his golden Lab, Journey, either.

One of the aides came down the corridor into the main area. "Looking for your grandfather?"

"Yes. He must be in his room." Kenia hurried toward the door, barely ajar. A more sociable man she'd never met. He never hid away, so he mustn't be feeling well. She tapped lightly on the door as she pushed it open. "Granddad?"

Sunshine streamed in the window, illuminating her grandfather as he sat, tall and straight, staring out the window, his leathery cheeks damp.

Kenia rushed around the bed, knelt beside his chair, and wrapped her arms around him. "Granddad? What's wrong? Aren't you feeling well?" Sure, he might be turning ninety-one this summer, but she wasn't ready to face a world without him. She never would be.

She felt the shudder pass through his body as his gnarled hand patted her back. "It's spring again."

That might be pushing it, although it had been pleasantly warm the past few days, at least for late February. Much of the winter's snow had melted, leaving mud and exposing brown grass.

"Is there anything green?" Granddad asked wistfully.

Kenia knew what he meant. "The crocuses are peeking through."

"It's time to start seedlings in the greenhouse. Is it alive in there?"

Granddad had passed the garden center on to Kenia's parents when he retired, but the love of growing things had never left him. Years — decades — had passed. Now Dad was nearly ready to pass the business on to her brother.

"Dad and Grady are keeping their crew busy. Maybe next week I can take you to see the greenhouses. They're keeping the temperatures just warm enough for the early bulbs."

She glanced at the large bouquet of daffodils and

tulips on the small table on the other side of Granddad. Mom had been by, then. She dropped off a new arrangement every week from Blossoms by the Akers, the flower shop Kenia would be learning to manage if it weren't for her allergies. She loved books, sure, but the family business ran deep in her veins. It just wasn't worth the nasal congestion, the itchy hives, the bleary eyes and aching throat.

"I'd like that. Maybe I can get my hands in the dirt."

Unlikely. Dad ran a tight ship at the garden center, and everything operated like clockwork. But... wait. "I know, Granddad. We can go to the old greenhouses. Some of the farmers market vendors are starting seedlings for the summer season, and Maisie is gathering her volunteer army to grow food for Corinna's Cupboard again."

Maisie might be only eleven, but the kid was a force to be reckoned with when it came to her passion for feeding the hungry. That her new stepdad operated a soup kitchen and food pantry for the homeless had only added fuel to her flames.

Granddad frowned. "Maisie?"

"You remember her," Kenia said softly. "She comes in sometimes with Joanna and Grady. Joanna brings her nephews and Maisie."

A glazed look crossed his eyes, and Kenia's heart clenched. She treasured every moment of clarity, but it had been a hard winter. How could he not remember the children? He loved their visits so much. Joanna's seven-year-old nephews, Evan and Oliver, never ceased to light up his face.

Kenia made a mental note to bring the kids herself if her sister-in-law was too busy, then pushed the thought aside. "The old greenhouses are a busy place, Granddad. The daycare is using one of them to teach the little ones where their food comes from. The after-school program is in there, too, testing if cabbages can keep growing all winter. The children love to pull fresh carrots for their snacks."

Granddad's gaze fixed hungrily on Kenia's face. He'd deeded his house, the greenhouses, and the town lot they sat on to Grace Fellowship in a living trust after he'd moved into Retro Village. Dad had built bigger, more modern greenhouses on the south end of Arcadia Valley when Kenia and Grady had just been kids, so the business had long ceased needing the older structures for its operations.

"Take me?" asked her grandfather.

The deep sadness in his eyes had been replaced by a glimmer of hope. How could she deny him? "I'll find out when it's a good time to drop by, and I'll check with the staff here to know when I can take you out. Last time I looked, the activity board was full of programs for you."

The old man grunted. "I don't want to be lifted into the swimming pool with a hoist and then hope I don't drown for half an hour. Wilbur and Amos like it, but I don't. The chlorine makes my skin dry and itchy."

Kenia chuckled. "It does the same to mine, but there are other activities." She brightened her voice. "Blake is in the common room right now with his dog. Want to go pet her?"

He scowled at her.

Guess not, then. But there was only so much more of this close proximity to the huge bouquet she could handle before she started sneezing. "I need to get going, Granddad, but I promise I'll get you out to the greenhouses real soon, okay?"

He was already back to staring out the window.

She pressed a kiss to his cheek, tiptoed out of the room, and nearly tripped over Journey. "Sorry, girl." She patted the large dog on the head and glanced up at Blake.

Blake gestured toward Granddad's room. "Would he like a visit?"

Kenia shook her head. "I don't think so, but it doesn't hurt to try. Hey, I've been curious about something."

The man angled his head and focused on her. "What's that?"

"How did you come up with the idea of bringing dogs into Retro for the residents? There are others who come, too, right? But you're the coordinator?"

He nodded. "I was involved in a dog therapy

program in Charleston before moving here. Journey and I both missed it, so I talked to the administrator and the activities coordinator to see if we could get something going here. It's worked out well."

"I'm sure it's a blessing to many of the residents. My granddad never had dogs. Said all they'd do was dig up his gardens."

Blake chuckled. "That would never do."

"You're right." Kenia laughed. "He was always so busy, so focused. Getting old has been rough on him, because he can't do all the stuff he used to do." She lowered her voice. "Between you and me, he was kind of crying a bit ago. He'd hate for me to tell anyone, but it's because he misses the gardens so much."

"Does he get out into the patio? Maybe he could putter there."

She grimaced. "The groundskeeper shot that down last summer, probably because Granddad wouldn't stop telling the workers what they were doing wrong."

Blake laughed. "I can see that wouldn't go over so well. Doesn't your family still own the garden center? Can't he visit sometimes on a day pass?"

"Yeah, he can. It's not the same, though. It's a really busy time for the business and he can't just do what he wants." Kenia shook her head. "I don't even know if he knows what he wants. Probably to just stare at a bean plant while it unfurls and grows in some kind of magic fast forward."

"It wouldn't hurt to talk to the administrator. Maybe they have another bit of land, not in the fenced patio, but somewhere else, where he could go. I mean, they're all about quality of life here. I'm sure Mr. Davis would help."

Another bit of land. Crazy, when the family already owned so much of it. She narrowed her eyes and stared at Blake, her mind whirling. "I think you just gave me an idea."

"Glad to help." He shot her a grin and then tapped on Granddad's door before pushing it open slightly. "Clarence? Would you like a visitor? Journey's here to see you."

Kenia didn't wait to hear the answer as she headed out of Frank Sinatra Pod and down the corridor to the main lobby.

Zane shifted restlessly on the chair in his boss's office. "You wanted to see me, Mr. Davis?" His mind scrambled over the past few weeks, but he couldn't think of anything he'd done wrong.

The fifty-something man shuffled a few papers to one side of his desk before looking up. "I did. I've got bad news for you, son. Your semi-annual review is coming up, and it's not looking good for keeping you on full time."

Zane's head reeled. "I'm sorry, sir. What can I do to make you change your mind?" Hadn't he been wracking his brain for new activities for the residents? Wheelchair bowling hadn't gone over as well as he'd hoped, but many of them loved Bingo.

"I know there are only so many hours in a day and that Arcadia Valley is a small town with limited amenities, but you need to find ways to get every resident involved in at least two activities a week."

"But there are fifty residents." That was one hundred activities in a forty-hour week for old people who napped a lot. Impossible.

"And some of them resist every effort to distract them. I know. Mrs. Black's knitting class is popular, but here's the thing." Mr. Davis folded his hands on the desk and looked straight at Zane. "Mrs. Black has been coming in once a week for years. She'll keep coming whether you put her on the schedule or not."

Zane bit his lip so he wouldn't burst out in protest and lose his job instantly.

"Blake Taylor has several volunteers bringing dogs in for the residents. Once again, it was his idea and he basically runs it. He'd come whether or not someone okayed the timeframe."

This was grossly unfair. How could he help it if the community was already chipping in? Wasn't that the goal? To keep the residents involved in their town instead of forgotten?

"Here's the thing, son. You need to come up with at least two or three solid ideas the residents will actually come out for on a weekly basis before the end of June. Events you are personally involved in operating, not just rubber-stamping." Mr. Davis held up his hand. "I know that sound unfair, but the board is looking for ways to cut costs, and your position is at the top of the list. The way it stands right now, we can put a clipboard at the front desk and volunteers can sign up to offer their activities without anyone overseeing it. It might get a bit messy at times, but it's a valid way to trim the budget."

Three brand new ideas? That he oversaw himself? Even researching them would be a killer. It wasn't like he could easily browse the internet to see what other senior facilities were doing.

"Do you have any questions?"

Zane slowly shook his head. "No, sir. I have four months to breathe new life into the program, or I'm gone. That's clear enough." A *lot* of new life.

"We might be able to keep you part-time."

Big help. He was twenty-nine years old with taxes to pay and a life to live. He'd just spent over two hundred bucks on a whim a couple of weeks ago. Obviously, he needed to be more careful, but he hadn't expected to stare the end of his job in the face.

A job he didn't even love, but one he desperately needed to keep.

Mr. Davis gathered a small pile of papers together.

"As it happens, I do have one idea for you. A relative of one of the residents came in yesterday asking if it might be possible to take her grandfather to the Grace Greenhouse project once or twice a week. You know the old greenhouses near Grace Fellowship are being used for various community activities. Here's some information about what they're doing there, as well as some other material about getting seniors involved in gardening." He held the pile toward Zane.

Mechanically, Zane accepted the papers. There was no picture on the top page to give him a clue, but it was full of words in small, bouncy type. Great. "Thanks, sir. I'll look these over and see what I can do."

Mr. Davis stood, signaling the end of the interview. "For what it's worth, son, I'm rooting for you. I think you've brought value to Retro Village, but I do understand the board's budget concerns. They wanted to give you to the end of the first quarter, but I argued that five weeks wasn't long enough to turn things around. I'll do whatever I can to help you out."

Did that include reading the stack of papers to him out loud? Zane squelched the snort that wanted to erupt. Not a chance. One hint that the event coordinator could barely read would get him out on his ear instantly. It had happened before, even on sites where it didn't really matter if he could navigate pages of text to do his job. Couldn't read? Good luck, buddy. See you down the trail.

"I appreciate the head's up and the support, sir." Zane rose and tucked the papers under his arm. "I'll do my best not to let you down."

He strode out to his truck and dumped the stack into the passenger seat. Gardening for seniors. He knew nothing about growing plants and cared even less. Well, that was about to change. Gardening was going to be his hobby. No, his passion. It was going to ooze out of his every pore and infect everyone around him.

Just as soon as he got back to the house, flipped on his laptop, and began to scour YouTube. He could learn anything there. Anything at all.

Even reading?

Zane shoved the key in the ignition and started the truck. There wasn't any way to learn to read from a video. There wasn't any way for him to learn to read at all.

Wistfulness overtook him at the memory of Tony's nose in a book every time his housemate had a few free minutes. There were paperbacks in every room, the tablet on the table, and outdoors magazines with great photos in the bathroom. How could the guy possibly enjoy watching words and letters wiggle all over?

How about Kenia, and all the people who bought books from her? Or the library patrons? People seemed to *love* reading. It was crazy.

And it wasn't for him.

Chapter 4

"NOW, DOES THIS EVER TAKE me back to my childhood." Kenia breathed deeply of the moist, warm air in the greenhouse, filling her lungs with the loamy aroma. She pointed to the far corner. "I'd take my dolls underneath that potting table and get Granddad's workers to pull some of the tall plants in front of it. It was like a playhouse for me."

Her friend Evelyn Kujak, the manager of the Grace Greenhouse Project, chuckled. "I can just see it. Didn't water ever drip on you?"

"I don't remember. They might have put garbage bags underneath the trays of seedlings." Kenia shrugged. "I played under there for hours at a time. When I got a little older, the dolls stayed in the chest in my room and books came along. I was Mary Lennox discovering the miracles of secret gardens with Dickon; I was Heidi playing with Peter's goats on the Alm; I was Ramona Quimby running wild on Klickitat Street."

"When did your parents move the business to the bigger site? I'm surprised you have so many memories here."

"When I was really little, but Granddad did a lot of the potting for them until I was ten or twelve. We'd come here after school, and Grady helped out with the transplanting, learning the systems and all that. He's five years older than me. I guess everyone figured he was old enough to work and, besides, he was interested even then. I lived in my own little world, and they let me."

Her own little world. She still lived there, surrounded by knights in shining armor rescuing damsels in distress. She'd told Perlita the truth — she read a variety of genres, but only if they were woven with a wide ribbon of romance. What good was any world without gallant, handsome men who swept women off their feet, brought flowers, and kissed passionately? She wasn't allergic to fictional blossoms.

"So that's how it started." Evelyn poked Kenia's ribs. "Your love affair with books."

"Aunt Irene was ready to step in when it turned out I couldn't work with flowers every day without full-on sinus congestion and welts of hives. Page Turners is a perfect fit for me."

"Well, I'm glad you can enjoy coming in here without reacting. It's because we're organic, right?"

"Yeah. My parents didn't figure it was economically

viable to run the commercial business without all the pesticides, herbicides, and supplements. Anyway, it's nice to see this place operating the way Granddad used to."

"It's better for the kids in the daycare program and for the community gardens. Well, it's better for everyone."

Kenia laughed. "I believe it. Try to convince my parents, my mom especially. Apparently you can't run a flower shop without perfect blossoms, and those have to be micro-managed."

"I've heard all about it from Bryanna."

Sometimes Kenia forgot that Evelyn's sister-in-law was the new manager at Blossoms, training to take over the business when Mom retired. Taking the position her parents had planned for their daughter.

"She says Grady is researching organic methods, or at least more natural."

"Too little, too late," Kenia replied. "But it's honestly okay. Aunt Irene and I get along perfectly, and she and Uncle Gerald never had kids of their own. Mom is sometimes a little jealous of how close I am to Dad's sister, but Mom worked long hours all my life. I'd have been a latchkey kid if not for Granddad and Aunt Irene."

"I'm so glad Maisie escaped that, for the most part. I'm not sure how I managed, sometimes. God definitely took care of us."

"And brought you to Ben. Now that's a perfect

happily-ever-after if I ever heard one."

Evelyn shook her head. "Trust me, there have been adjustments for all three of us. I'd been forced to be very self-sufficient for years. Letting Ben take care of things has been quite a process. It's also been hard for him, at times, having Maisie and me in the home he built for his first wife and daughter. It hasn't been all sunshine and roses."

"La la la." Kenia stuck her fingers in her ears and closed her eyes. "That's not what I want to hear at all."

Her friend laughed. "Still true. Oh, it's definitely worth it, but we happen to be imperfect people who wake up every morning and sometimes wonder what we were thinking."

"Oh, wow. I don't want to know. I'll take my rose-colored glasses every time."

There were a few seconds of silence. "Like with Jonah?" asked Evelyn quietly.

Ouch. "What's that supposed to mean?"

"You knew he was in love with Gloria even while you were dating. Everyone knew."

"He said he was over her." He'd lied, apparently. It was more like he'd been trying to *get* over her, since she'd pushed him away at every turn.

"You set yourself up for heartbreak."

"He's a great guy. A solid Christian, hard-working, cute, funny."

Evelyn held up both hands. "No argument."

"And in love with a married woman." That might be what rankled most.

"You can't blame him for that. Gloria didn't tell anyone she'd been married. Not even Serena knew, and they've been best friends for ages."

"I know. I know. All I want is a man who loves me like crazy, you know?"

"That's not all."

Kenia sighed. "No, you're right." She held up her hand and began ticking off fingers. "I want a man who loves God with all his heart. Who loves me almost as much. Who can cook, because I sure can't. Who treats me like a princess, but still lets me be a tomboy. Who..."

Evelyn's eyes were focused on something beyond Kenia, and she wore a bemused expression on her face. "Can I help you with something?"

Kenia whirled. The guy from the benefit concert who'd come by the bookstore. The guy who'd asked her out, and she'd turned him down. The guy she hadn't been able to get out of her mind in the ten days since.

That guy stood not three feet behind her, shifting from one foot to the other, his gaze catching on hers as a dull red crept up his unshaven cheeks.

No doubt matching the color of her own. Good grief, what had he overheard? Her litany of qualities in her dream man. She'd barely gotten started, but still. She must have sounded like a moonstruck teenager, not an adult businesswoman.

"Hi. Zane, right?" As though she didn't remember every one of the few words that had passed between them, but someone had to break the silence, and it didn't seem like he'd be the one.

He pulled him together visibly and looked over at Evelyn. "Yes, Zane Russell. You're Evelyn? The manager of this greenhouse?"

Of course, he wasn't here because he wanted to see her. If he wanted to see Kenia, he'd come back to Page Turners and redeem the certificate he'd bought. But what on earth did he want with Evelyn? No way was Kenia leaving now. She was far too curious.

"I'm pleased to meet you, Zane. Yes, I'm Evelyn Kujak. What can I do for you?"

Zane angled himself so the fiery-haired beauty wasn't directly in his line of vision. He couldn't let himself get distracted, not when his job was on the line. "I was wondering if you could explain what these greenhouses are for? How you decide what kind of programs to run."

"Sure. This lot belonged to Clarence Akers, who's now a resident of Retro Village. He signed the property to Grace Fellowship, the church just down the block, in a living trust to be used for the betterment of the community in Jesus' name."

"Wait. Who owned it?" Surely he'd misheard.

"Clarence Akers." Evelyn gestured to Kenia. "You've met Kenia before, I take it? Clarence is her grandfather."

Click. Of course. He glanced at Kenia. "I work at Retro Village. Your grandfather is one of my favorites."

It was no more than the truth, but she blinked at him. "I haven't run into you there. I drop by to visit him at least twice a week."

His heart bumped. He hadn't seen her there, either. "I'm the activities coordinator, so I work with the residents of all the pods. Take them on outings, that sort of thing."

"That's great." Kenia seemed like she had more to say, but she glanced between him and her friend and closed her mouth.

Her very pretty mouth.

Zane turned back to Evelyn. "You were saying?"

"About the programs. Clarence's house has been remodeled into a children's center. Both the daycare and the after-school program use the second greenhouse. We have a variety of things going on in this one. Some farmers market vendors start their seedlings in here to get a head start on the growing season. We also start many plants for the large gardens you likely saw when you drove in. The food grown there is split between Corinna's Cupboard and the volunteers."

The potting tables lining the gravel paths beyond

him all had trays on them, little green shoots poking through black dirt in small compartments. "So, you're full up then."

"Maybe, and maybe not. Did you have something in mind?"

He had... until he'd discovered the connection between Kenia and the old man in Sinatra Pod. Now he wasn't so sure. He didn't want to sound like a stalker. On the other hand, he needed a job, and history reminded him they weren't easy to come by for a guy who struggled with reading. Best to focus on keeping the one he had.

"I'm always on the lookout for new activities for the residents. I was reminded recently that, in the old days, many of them had gardens and maybe they would enjoy puttering again. Do you think there's a chance we could put something together?"

Kenia put her hand on his arm. "Granddad was pretty wistful the other day when I stopped by. I'd love to see something like this happen for his sake."

She was so touchy-feely. Was a demonstrative guy on her list? He couldn't believe what he'd overheard. Did women talk like that all the time? Quinn had said Kenia was seeing someone. Zane had figured that's why she turned him down. It was easier than believing he'd bungled up so badly she wasn't interested, but now he wondered. In the bit he'd overheard, it didn't sound like she was dating.

Her hand left a chilly spot when she removed it. He looked at her. She'd love to see this program happen? Then it would. If Evelyn didn't agree, he'd find some other way, but nothing would stop him now.

Evelyn chuckled, and Zane forced himself to look over at her. "If Clarence wants it, I don't see why we can't work something out. If it weren't for his generous trust, none of this would be here. Everything would have been torn down for a row of condos by now."

From the corner of his eye, Zane caught Kenia's shudder. Preserving family history obviously meant a lot to her. He added that to his mental list.

"Do you have a proposal I can take to the board?" Evelyn asked. "We meet tomorrow evening. I'm sure it will fly through, but we do need to go through the proper channels."

Proposal. That meant writing. That meant knowing what he was doing. It also meant a headache, but he'd do it. "I don't have anything firm right now. I was hoping you'd have time for a discussion, if you were open to the idea, and guide me. I'm not really a gardener." Much as it pained him to admit it in present company.

"I don't have any experience working with the elderly." Evelyn checked her watch. "And I need to pick up my daughter from school in a few minutes. Zane, why don't you tell Kenia what you have in mind? She'll be able to give you good direction, and the two of you can put together something for the board. You've got time, don't you, Kenia?"

Evelyn's body language said she was telling the truth, but there was more to it. She couldn't be playing matchmaker, could she? No way. She didn't know Zane from a hole in the ground. She couldn't know that Zane did, in fact, meet Kenia's requirement number one: a man who loved the Lord.

This project was run by Grace Fellowship, and Zane had been attending Arcadia Valley Community Church. It was bigger, with two services, making it easy to disappear into the crowd. Tony had been coming to Grace and told Zane he thought he'd like it. Maybe this was a good time to accompany his friend.

Unless, by the end of the next hour, Kenia didn't seem ready to act on the spark of interest he was sure he'd seen in her. A spark that matched the one in his own heart. See? He could do the romancey thing. He was already halfway there.

"What do you say, Kenia? Is there a place here where we can talk for a bit, or would you like to grab a coffee somewhere?" Oops. Maybe too much, since she'd turned down a date last time.

"I've got paperwork for tomorrow night spread out all over my desk," Evelyn put in. "You'd probably be better off somewhere else."

Kenia narrowed her gaze at her friend.

For a long moment, Zane was sure she'd say no.

She turned back to him. "Okay, I can meet you at the Jukebox. Did you bring a notebook?"

Yikes, she didn't sound too happy about it. Zane made a show of patting his pockets. "No, sorry. I didn't think of it."

"I'll stop by Page Turners and grab one then. Meet you there in ten."

"Sounds good." Perfect, actually. If she brought the notebook, she'd expect to be the one writing in it. With any luck, he could get her to write the proposal, too, without suspecting a thing.

Because he was pretty sure her list didn't include a man who didn't read. *Couldn't* read, if he were being honest... but that was one topic where honesty had never proven to be the best policy.

Chapter 5

KENIA SLIPPED INTO THE BOOTH where Zane waited for her and set the spiral-bound notebook on the table. Why did he have to look so darn enticing with his tousled hair? She wanted to sweep the strands aside and get a better look at his startling dark eyes.

She patted the notebook, where hearts and flowers entwined around a stack of books, crowned with a sleeping cat and a teacup. "I've been looking for an excuse to pick up one of these. Thanks for giving me one."

Zane glanced down and then back to her face, like he couldn't stop looking at her. "Glad to be of service." A grin lifted one end of his mouth, poking a dimple.

No. Way. How had she not noticed the dimple before? Because she hadn't given him occasion to smile, probably. And she still shouldn't. She was getting over a broken heart and needed to give herself time.

A waitress stopped at the end of their booth. "Can I get you a menu?"

Kenia shook her head. "Not for me, thanks. I'd like a mocha milkshake." She looked at Zane's surprised expression. "I know summer is a distant dream, but I can't resist."

He grinned and turned to the waitress. "What flavors do you have?"

She pointed at a chalkboard above the till and began to recite. "Vanilla, chocolate, strawberry—"

"Strawberry sounds good."

"Coming right up!" The waitress bustled away, her poodle skirt whirling around her knees.

"Strawberry, huh? I would have pegged you for a butterscotch kind of guy."

He shrugged, not quite meeting her eyes. "I like nearly anything."

Odd way to put it, but it didn't matter. She wasn't interested in him, so it didn't matter what his idiosyncrasies were. Okay, she could *become* interested, but she was giving herself time. Time to figure out what was wrong with her that Jonah couldn't fall in love with her. His rejection stung. It wasn't fair to any guy she started dating if she compared him to Jonah all the time.

She opened the notebook and poised her favorite turquoise gel pen over it. "Tell me what you've got in mind."

Zane leaned on the table and pursed his lips.

Don't look at his lips. Kenia stared down at the unlined page.

"I don't really know anything about gardening. From my end, I only know the residents and their schedule. We could fit in one visit a week. Is an hour long enough for them to enjoy the greenhouse, or do we need longer? Of course, the longer the time period, the fewer residents will sign up for it since some of them tire easily."

Kenia tapped her pen against her chin. "An hour is good, probably. It might even be too long. There might not be anything to do some days. I mean, once seeds are planted, there's not much to do for a while but water them."

He sighed. "Maybe the whole thing is a bad idea."

"No, I think you're on to something. I know Granddad misses watching plants grow like crazy. I found him staring out his window at the gardens the other day with tears trickling down his cheeks."

Two tall glasses clunked onto the table, one pink, one brown, both topped with a swirl of whipped cream. A metal straw protruded from each. "Can I get you anything else?"

"This is perfect, thanks." Zane smiled up at the waitress as he reached for his glass.

His fingers brushed Kenia's then his gaze swung to meet hers.

Why was his touch so electrifying? Why were his eyes so riveting? She hadn't felt this connected to Jonah, who'd been the perfect guy for her — at least if she discounted that he'd been in love with someone else the whole time — so it was silly to feel this attraction to a guy she didn't know.

Ridiculous, even. Obviously her instincts and feelings were completely untrustworthy. She'd simply ignore them.

Zane pulled his shake to his side of the table and put his lips around the straw, his gaze never leaving hers.

Oh, yeah, just ignore him. That'd be sooo easy.

Kenia forced herself to focus on her milkshake and took a sip. "Great, as usual. How's the strawberry?"

"Very good. I can't remember when I last had a milkshake in winter."

"Tomorrow's March first. It's almost spring."

Zane grinned in his lopsided way. "True. And that's why we're here, I guess." He poked his chin toward the notebook in front of her. "To get the residents out where they can experience the changing of the seasons."

"Right." He might've asked her out two weeks ago. He might cause her insides to quiver with a single flash of that dimple, but they did have a task to accomplish. "Okay, so we've got an hour a week, but it will be hard to fill it consistently. Were you thinking morning or afternoon?"

He frowned thoughtfully. "Mornings are pretty busy.

The hairdresser comes in on Mondays, and some of the ladies won't want to miss that. Mrs. Black has a knitting class on Tuesday mornings. We have carpet bowling on Wednesdays, swimming on Thursdays..." His voice trailed off.

"Dinner at Retro is at five, so everyone would need to be back by four-thirty, right? Could we try for three o'clock? If it was Monday or Tuesday, I could help out. Those are the days my aunt is in the bookstore, so I'm more flexible."

Zane nodded. "Tuesday might be good. Afternoons are trickier because of the naps, but everyone should be awake and raring to go by two-thirty."

Tuesday 3:00-4:00. She wrote it in her notebook and added a flourish beside the words. A sudden thought struck her. "Oh! I know. That's right when the kids come for after-school care. How about integrating the seniors with the kids? It might benefit everyone."

He frowned at her. "But..."

"No, really. Our society segregates age groups so much. I'll talk to Alaina. She runs the kids' programs, and she used to be my housemate before getting married last Christmas."

Call Alaina became embellished with swirls and flowers.

"If you're sure."

"Granddad loves Alaina's stepsons. They're a lively pair. In fact, everyone in Frank Sinatra brightens up when one of us takes Oliver and Evan in for a visit."

The familiar spark of jealousy still poked Kenia. Not that she'd been interested in Cameron Kraus, the twins' father. Not that she'd wanted to take on raising those boys. It was just... why was everyone around her falling in love and getting married and maybe soon having babies, and she was as single as the day she'd been born? Yep, the only men in her life were her grandfather, her dad, and her brother.

The man across from her shook his head as though he could read her mind. Maybe he could, in which case she'd better zip those negative thoughts into a back corner.

"How would that even work?" asked Zane.

"When there are tasks like planting or transplanting or weeding, they can work alongside the kids. I'm sure Alaina will think it's a great idea." She underlined Alaina's name in the notebook and drew a puffy cloud around it. "When there's nothing happening in the greenhouse, maybe the residents and kids can enjoy crafts together. Or, I know! Maybe the seniors can read to the kids, or the kids can even read to the seniors. They always need practice."

Why wasn't Zane catching her vision? He stared at her like she was from outer space. She talked faster, sketching a stack of books on the page. "Books and plants. Now that's a great combination..."

Zane stared, mesmerized, as Kenia chattered on and wrote things in her notebook. From upside down, he could tell some of it was pictures, but even what appeared to be words seemed to be decorated. He gave his head a shake, but it didn't clear his vision.

His only hope now lay in her creating the proposal. If she tore that page out and handed it to him, there'd be no way to decipher the thing. But, since she'd promised to call her friend, she'd probably take care of the rest of it, too.

You need to come up with at least two or three solid ideas... events you are personally involved in operating, not just approving. Mr. Davis's words rang in his ears.

Before that visit to the principal's office — for that's what the summons had felt like — he would've been happy to let Kenia run with it. Sure, he was interested in her, but not enough to stick around when things got to the reading level. He wasn't in her league, and there was no point in pretending she'd ever go for a loser like him.

Lord, why am I so stupid? Why can't I do what millions of little kids learn how to do with no problem?

"What do you think?" Kenia looked at him expectantly.

"Uh. Can you sum that up?"

She laughed. "Sorry. I guess I got my passion on."

Zane couldn't help grinning back. "So Tuesdays at three. I'll have to make sure the handi-bus is available then, but I think it is. You're going to check with your friend..."

"Alaina Kraus." Kenia glanced at her watch. "She gets off at six tonight, so I'll give her a call this evening and run it by her."

"The board meeting is tomorrow."

"Yeah." Kenia scrunched her cute nose. "That doesn't leave a lot of time. I can email you what I have after talking to Alaina, and you can put your own spin on it and drop it by to Evelyn? If you have a printer available."

Relief swept him to his toes. "That should work." He could get the computer to read her email to him. "We've got a printer. One of the guys in my house needs to print stuff for his business all the time."

She angled a glance toward him. "Who's your roommate?"

"There's three of us. Quinn Lawson runs—"

"Snake River Tours! He's my friend Jamie's brother. I want to do one of his trips sometime."

Zane filed the information away. "The other guy in my house is Tony Santoro. He's a chef at his uncle's restaurant in Twin Falls."

"Oh, that's so cool. I bet you guys eat well."

The words he'd overheard rang into his mind. *I want a man who can cook, because I sure can't.*

He wasn't that great, either, but he did have a knack for sniffing the spices and finding flavors that seemed compatible. Nothing like the stuff Tony threw together, though. "We take turns, depending on our schedules."

Kenia smiled. "If I get another housemate, she'll need to know how to cook. I'm hopeless, and Alaina wasn't much better. She and Cameron took cooking classes together last fall. So did my brother and his wife, actually."

Zane couldn't help teasing. "Sounds like you should have joined them."

"Going solo didn't sound like that much fun." Her nose wrinkled. "I probably should have. I come by it honestly, though. My mother can barely boil water. They've always hired a cook, and my Aunt Irene practically has a table with her name on it at El Corazon. I bet she eats Mexican five nights a week."

Eating out had its own challenges, like reading a menu. Zane nearly always went for the special to simplify his life. At least at the Food Mart he could see the product he was buying. "El Corazon has great food."

"Yeah, they freshened everything a couple of years ago. It was pretty old school before Molly came back to Arcadia Valley and shook up the menu." Kenia laughed. "And got back together with Javier Quintana. But I guess you didn't know them before, since you didn't grow up here." She left that with almost a question.

He shook his head. "I visited my grandparents here

every summer, but they've been gone for a few years now."

"I'm sorry to hear that. Were you close? I know I'll miss Granddad desperately when his time comes."

"As close as I was to anyone." Grandma at least hadn't lectured him all the time about trying harder, about not being distracted so easily, about goofing off. It wasn't like Zane had been trying to be a horrid lazy kid and embarrass his ultra-educated parents. The less he saw of them, the better.

"Is that why you work at Retro Village?"

Huh? Zane blinked at her. Oh. Let her think what she wanted. He wasn't about to tell her how hard it was for a non-reader to get a job. Any job at all. "It may have played into my decision, I guess. Not consciously."

"Well, I'm thankful for you." Her hand covered his for a few seconds. "I'm thankful Retro Village has so many staff members that really care about providing quality care for the residents. There are horror stories on TV from time to time about elder abuse in some facilities, and it's just not something we're worried about at Retro."

His hand tingled where her fingers brushed his before she grabbed up her pen and began doodling again. If he'd been quicker, he could have turned his palm over and... no, it had just been an impulse on her part. The touch didn't likely mean anything to her. He'd asked her out, and she'd turned him down. Other than finding out she was, in fact, not dating anyone, nothing had changed. Besides, keeping his secret would be difficult if she got too close.

Did that mean he'd never marry and have a family? All because he couldn't read? But the alternative was owning up to his problems. Since no one could solve them, and he couldn't live with pity, that wasn't a great solution, either. He'd have to just brace up and learn to enjoy his life the way it was.

Empty.

Chapter 6

J 'M GLAD YOU CAME BY to pick up these books." Kenia gave her friend a big smile. "But, I have to say, having them sit on the counter for two days has resulted in several more orders for the entire series."

Constance's face brightened as she touched the top book. "Portia will be so happy. We're having her ninth birthday party at the YMCA on Saturday. She's excited, of course — we've invited half a dozen of her little friends — but she'll be most excited to get this gift from her papa."

"Felipe is off on Saturday?" Constance's husband was one of the town's police officers and, while he doted on his five daughters, Kenia couldn't quite imagine him wrangling other people's kids at a birthday party. Maybe that's because her own dad would never have done it.

"He traded a shift with Gloria so he could come." Constance glanced down then met Kenia's gaze. "How are you doing?"

Kenia didn't have to ask what Constance was referring to, especially not with Gloria's name slipping casually into the conversation. "Oh, I'm doing fine." She'd like to add that she and Jonah had just been friends, that she'd never had any expectations from their brief relationship, but it wouldn't quite be true. She'd burned a piece of paper where she'd practiced signing Kenia Baxter, after all. She hadn't needed to keep the reminder or let anyone else discover it.

"I'm glad to hear it. You know you two were an unlikely pair."

"Oh, I'm not so sure." She forced a tinkling laugh. "A man who lives to cook and bake? Isn't that every woman's dream?"

Constance chuckled. "And here I've always heard that food was the way to a *man's* heart."

"In today's world, it can go either way." Kenia shook her head. "You know what the problem is with our breakup? He and Gloria are still miserable, still not dating. Whoever would have thought she had a husband stashed away she wasn't divorced from?"

"I'm sure we were all shocked."

Kenia glanced around the bookstore to double check that no one had come in without her hearing the bells, but they were alone. She lowered her voice anyway. "Why didn't they get divorced? They've been apart for years."

"She didn't feel it was right for her to be the one pursuing divorce, and Frank never mentioned it."

"I mean, I'm not advocating easy come, easy go, but when there's no hope of reconciliation? Doesn't a person have to get on with their life? Look at Cameron. Lisa left him several years ago and sent divorce papers. At least he was free when Alaina came into his life." Unlike Gloria, who was still tied to a man she hadn't seen in forever.

"Gloria and Frank split because she became a Christian, and he wanted nothing to do with that. She'd hoped and prayed he'd see his need of a Savior and turn his life around."

"After eight years?"

Constance shook her head. "One day at a time. It adds up. You may not understand her decision, but she did what she felt was right."

"I'd have thought that once she knew she was falling in love with Jonah, she'd have realized there was no hope of getting back together with Frank." Kenia held up both hands. "I know, I know. It's none of my business." Only... it sort of had been. Didn't the six weeks she and Jonah dated count for anything? Realizing how deep his feelings ran for Gloria, even after he found out she was married, had sliced Kenia's legs out from under her.

With a start, she realized the grief was gone, and she was left puzzling over Gloria's decisions. Why couldn't the policewoman see what she was still pushing away in Jonah, who was practically the perfect man, who adored her — all for a bum who'd never valued her at all? Kenia wanted to shake her. *Don't cling to the past! Grab the man! Reach for the future!*

"Good morning, Constance." Aunt Irene's heels clicked on the hardwood floor as she approached from the back room. "And happy birthday to your little mermaid princess."

Constance laid her wallet on the counter. "Thank you, Irene. Portia's so excited. And having the rest of her favorite series will be better than the icing on her cake."

Kenia rang up the order while Irene bagged the books. After Constance waved goodbye, Irene turned to Kenia.

"I told your granddad what you've managed to pull off with greenhouse excursions, and he sat there and cried. He couldn't stop smiling."

Kenia had wanted to tell him herself, not that she'd really done anything other than facilitate Zane's idea and run it by Alaina and Evelyn. Oh, and write up the proposal and forward it to him for the board. Okay, so she had helped quite a bit. "It was Zane's idea. I'd only thought of getting Granddad out on his own, but Zane had the vision for it to be a regular, official Retro Village outing."

Irene's pencil-thin eyebrows pulled together. "Zane?"

"Zane Russell. He's the activities coordinator at Retro. I told you about our meeting."

"Right. I'd missed his name. I thought the coordinator there was a woman."

"Not anymore." Oh, so definitely not female. Zane's rugged good looks, his muscular build, his perpetual five-o'clock shadow, his musky cologne, combined to be the epitome of masculinity.

"I'm glad you can do this for your grandfather and that it will benefit other residents, as well, but that brings up something else I wanted to talk to you about."

"Okay?" Had she been taking too much time off? Been too chatty with the customers? Maybe Irene had overheard her probing Constance for more information about Gloria and Frank. That might've qualified as gossip.

"We've talked about my retirement in general terms over the years, but the time is coming soon, Kenia. It's my hope you're interested in buying Page Turners in the next few months. By the end of the year at the latest. I can't afford to give it to you, but I'll definitely sell it to you for considerably less than market value. What do you say?"

Kenia's mind reeled. "You're not even sixty!"

Her aunt chuckled. "No, but it's coming, and I want to travel. Nancy Poncetta and I have been talking about spending the upcoming winter in Spain, where her family is from. Her cousin has offered us their cottage on the Mediterranean."

"Sounds idyllic."

Irene grinned. "That's what I thought. She's always been a good friend of mine, but we've grown closer since her husband passed away. So, about Page Turners. We can do this one of two ways. My preference is to sell you everything: the business and the building, but if you don't want the hassle of owning commercial real estate, I can try to sell it separately."

"There'd be a chance the new owner wouldn't want to lease to a bookstore."

"Hard to imagine, but true. Especially with the other storefront vacant right now, a new owner might want to combine the two and have one larger retail space."

Something Kenia had urged her aunt to do over the past couple of years herself. Expand the bookstore, put in a coffee bar, create a space where local writers could gather and local art be displayed. Wait. If she bought everything, she could do this herself.

If she could afford it. Irene hadn't figured she'd double the income from Page Turners with Kenia's ideas. There was more money to be made leasing the second storefront to another business, but since the kids' consignment shop had closed — the third business in as many years to vacate the location — maybe it was worth considering.

Kenia eyed her aunt speculatively. "I think I need some numbers and then time to figure out possibilities."

"By which you mean pray about it."

"Of course. That's part of the decision making process."

"Glad to hear it." Irene nodded. "I'll give Max Martinez a call and get him to assess the value both ways. If you decide not to go for the real estate, I'll have him list it."

Ideas and possibilities exploded in Kenia's mind. Could she pull this off?

Zane stood on the sidewalk and stared up the steps to the Arcadia Valley Library. The imposing concrete steps of the classic brick structure epitomized the difficulties he'd found with reading. Sure, a sign pointed to wheelchair access from the parking lot behind the building. If only there were similar things for guys like him to access words.

Maybe he should just be thankful for YouTube. He'd learned a lot about gardening already, but he needed more information. He swallowed hard. Books had information. Libraries had books. He could do this.

Slowly he mounted the steps and opened the ornate

wooden door set with stained glass windows. It swung open silently on oiled hinges, ushering him into a vestibule with coat hooks on one side and a community bulletin board on the other, some of the posters with pictures on them.

One caught his attention. An older man sat with a younger man, an open book on the table before them. Zane squinted at the large letters. Adult lite-something classes. He worked harder on the middle word. L-i-t-e-r-a-c-y. Lite racy? Didn't sound good. Below the image he made out the words, *Ask for Arthur*. Then there was a phone number.

Whatever that was all about.

He took a deep breath and faced the space. A woman sitting behind a large desk glanced up and smiled at him. "Hi there. Welcome to Arcadia Valley Library. Is this your first visit?"

It must be obvious. Zane nodded. "I'm looking for some books on gardening. Books for kids. With pictures."

She rose to her feet. "Sure, I can help you with that. The children's section is right through here. I'm Charlotte Delis, by the way. I'm the head librarian."

So many tall banks of books. He'd thought the bookstore closed in on him. This was ten times worse. The shelving systems went on forever, hundreds and thousands of spines barricading knowledge behind their tiny titles. How could anyone find anything in here?

Charlotte gestured to a brightly lit area with shorter cases containing books of variable sizes. Several children sat on large cushions littering the floor, turning pages with colorful images.

Zane took in a long breath and released it.

"The gardening books are over here. My stepdaughter particularly likes this series." Charlotte pulled out a volume. "Elena is nine. How old are your children?"

"Uh." He couldn't very well tell her the book was for him. He took it from her and flipped it open. Too many words. He handed it back. "Younger than your daughter." So much younger they weren't even a gleam in his eye.

"All right." Her finger slid along the spines until she pulled out another volume. "How about this?"

A quick glance caused him to nod. "This looks better. Anything else you can recommend in this category?"

"Sure. It's part of a series." Charlotte gathered five more books into a stack. "Is there anything else I can help you find?"

Zane's head was already at the splitting point from a pounding headache. Whether it was the florescent lights overhead or the books looming around him, threatening to topple and crush him, he wasn't sure. "This is everything for today." He followed her back to the desk.

"You probably don't have a library card since it's

your first visit."

He should've known there'd be more to it than dashing out the door. "You're right."

Charlotte smiled at him. "I can get you set up. I just need your name, phone number, and address." She keyed into her computer then looked over, fingers poised for his information.

As he recited the data, his gaze penetrated a glass wall behind her where the older man from the photo sat at a table with a middle-aged woman, who leaned over a book, biting her lip. Her finger slid slowly across the page.

Zane shook his head. She looked a lot like he did when he was trying to decipher words.

Wait. Lite racy. Literacy? Was that old guy Arthur, teaching someone to read? Too bad it couldn't be Zane, but it wasn't that he didn't know the letters and what they sounded like. It was that the letters rolled in waves across the page like special effects in a movie. Even Arthur couldn't make them stand still, if he'd even believe Zane's dilemma. His teachers never had. They'd laughed at his vivid imagination and told him to try harder.

Yeah. He'd tried, but all the trying in the world hadn't made a difference.

"Here you go." Charlotte ran a book through a scanner and slid the stack across the desk to him. "These are due back in three weeks, and you're allowed fifteen books at a time. If your kids are really enjoying them, you can renew them once if no one is waiting for them. Welcome to Arcadia Valley, Zane. I hope we see you in the library regularly, and feel free to bring your children next time. We have regular story hours and reading clubs." She added a sheet of paper to the top of the books. "All the info is on there, or you can look it up on our website."

Zane hadn't corrected her assumptions. In fact, he'd gone along with them. Guilt flooded him. Guilt that had gone hand-in-hand with his inability to decipher meaning from written words for most of his life. He'd guarded his secret ever since his parents and teachers had mocked his story years back. No way was he going to tell this stranger all his woes. Not a librarian, for sure. Not even one who could hook him up with literacy classes that wouldn't help.

He smiled at her with a nod, accepted the books, and headed for the door.

Lite racy indeed.

What a dumbbell.

Chapter 7

"ISS KENIA! MISS KENIA!"

She barely had time to brace herself before two bodies slammed into her in the church foyer. She wrapped an arm around each young boy's shoulder. "Hi, Evan. Hi, Oliver. How was Sunday school today?"

Seven-year-old Evan scowled. "Okay, I guess."

"Will you be our teacher again?" His twin peered up at her. "We liked when you were our teacher."

"Mrs. Wattenberg is old."

"She doesn't like kids."

Kenia crouched between the boys. "Hey, now. I'm sure she likes kids just fine or she wouldn't have volunteered to teach your class. What did you two do to her?"

The twins exchanged a look. "Nothing," mumbled Evan.

"Come on now. What happened?" Kenia hadn't taught this pair a couple of years ago without learning something about how their double-trouble mind worked.

"She called me Evan." Oliver rolled his eyes. "Anyone can see we don't look alike."

They didn't, not with Oliver's red-tinged hair and Evan's blond, nor were their personalities the same. Still, sometimes it was difficult to remember which name went with which face.

"All the kids laughed. Ophelia called us Olevan."

Kenia grinned and looked between the two disgruntled boys. "That's kind of cute. A good twin name."

Evan struck a kung fu pose. "We're not cute. We're warriors." He growled ferociously.

From behind her, Kenia heard Alaina's chuckle. "Are you trying to scare Miss Kenia?"

Oliver scowled indignantly. "No. We like her."

Kenia straightened and looked at the boys' stepmom, who was also her best friend. "I'm trying to learn what they do to people they don't like."

Alaina's eyebrows tented. "How did that come up?"

"No reason," Evan said quickly, peering past her.

"Where's Dad?"

She thumbed over her shoulder. "Talking to some new guys outside. I told him I'd come find you two since we're going to the Sunrise for lunch."

The twins high-fived each other. "Yeah."

Alaina shook her head and grinned at Kenia. "You'd think Cameron and I hadn't learned a thing about cooking from all those classes, the way those two cheer when we're eating out."

Kenia laughed. "I'd rather eat out than cook, myself."

"Want to join us? Or are you going to your parents' house?"

"Fran Martinez invited them for dinner today, so they're heading into Twin Falls. Mom was all apologetic, but I don't mind breaking tradition once in a while, especially since Grady and Joanna don't come every week anymore."

"So, come with us? Unless you want to eat your own cooking."

"Ha ha. Very funny. You weren't my roommate for six months without knowing I'm more likely to poison myself than anything else. The Sunrise sounds great. I love their Eggs Benny. Besides, I hardly ever see you anymore now that you're a married woman and all that."

Alaina practically glowed with happiness. Kenia had never really been attracted to Cameron — the rambunctious twins might have cured her of any inclination — but she couldn't deny he was good for her friend.

The boys stampeded toward the door, dodging old Mrs. Bennett, who shook her cane at them.

Alaina linked her arm with Kenia's and leaned on her shoulder with a sigh. "Let's go out for dessert some evening. Maybe to L'Aubergine. I could use a break from the high-testosterone life."

"Not all sunshine and roses?"

"I wouldn't say that." Her friend's lips curved in a secretive Mona Lisa smile. "Cameron is all that and more. And I adore Oliver and Evan. You know I do. But both my brain and body have trouble staying ahead of them. Trying to keep up isn't enough."

All that and more, huh? Kenia didn't want to know.

Alaina towed her across the church foyer, and Kenia avoided eye contact with Jonah's sister-in-law Ursula. Jonah himself was nowhere to be seen, which was just as well. Gloria attended Arcadia Valley Community Church when she wasn't on duty, so at least Kenia didn't have to worry about running into Jonah's would-be love.

March sunshine cast a welcome warmth as Kenia exited the building onto the sidewalk that curved toward the parking area. Parents herded kids toward cars, while others chatted in small groups. Up ahead, she spotted Cameron and two other men. The one with his back to her had broad shoulders and messy brown hair in need of a cut.

Her eyes narrowed. Zane Russell? Had he been in church? She hadn't noticed him. Hadn't expected him to be a church-goer at all. She tugged on Alaina's arm. "Who's Cameron talking to?"

"The shorter guy is Tony Santoro. He's a chef at Italiana in Twin Falls, and he taught one of our cooking classes last fall. Seems like a nice guy." Alaina raised her eyebrows at Kenia. "Cute. Single. And a chef."

"No more chefs." Although there had been some distinct benefits.

Alaina chuckled. "You *need* a chef. Just someone other than Jonah."

Kenia shook her head. "I'm over it." And she was, mostly. She'd be *more* over it if Gloria filed for divorce so she and Jonah could actually get engaged or at least date. As it was, Kenia had been thrown over for the ghost of might-have-been, and that still kind of irked. Wait. She'd been the one to break it off. She could hold her head up high.

"Don't know the other guy," Alaina mused as they approached.

At that instant, the trio turned toward them. Cameron's gaze warmed as he reached for Alaina and slid his arm around her waist. "I'd like you to meet my wife, Alaina. Alaina, this is Tony's friend Zane Russell."

"Pleased to meet you. Nice to see you again, Tony. This is my friend Kenia Akers."

Tony extended his hand. "Hi, Kenia. Any friend of Alaina's is a friend of mine."

Was the guy *flirting* with her? She shook his hand but glanced at Zane, who hung back, that lock of hair partially covering his eyes. "We meet again."

He tossed her a quick grin and nod.

"Shall we head over to the Sunrise?" asked Cameron. "Tony and Zane are joining us, and so are Joanna and Grady. You, too, Kenia?"

"Um..." Oh, why not? She'd already agreed to come. The men just didn't know it. "Sounds fun."

Alaina whirled away from Cameron's arm. "Where are the twins?"

Zane watched Tony hold out a chair for Kenia inside the café. He should've been faster. Now he was destined for the sidelines. Tony met Kenia's wish list. A Christian, a gentleman, and even a chef. Kenia hadn't gotten around to wishing for an avid reader in the conversation he'd overheard, but it would have been coming. Tony certainly fit that bill, too.

Not Zane. He might have had a moment of bravado on Valentine's Day in the Bigby family's barn when he'd thrown caution to the wind. Might have had something to do with the guy on stage crooning love songs and then proposing to his sweetheart in front of hundreds of people.

He'd come back to Earth since and remembered who he was. The guy who always came in second place, if he were lucky. Otherwise, he was at the end of the line.

When Kenia mentioned Page Turners, Tony's face lit with excitement. He rattled off some of his favorite authors. Of course, Kenia had read their books and knew what was coming next. Joanna and Alaina chimed in, while Cameron squirted ketchup on the boys' scrambled eggs.

Even the sausage and kale chowder tasted little better than cardboard. Butter melting in rivulets on sourdough biscuits did nothing to entice him.

Why? Why couldn't he fit in?

"What's your favorite genre, Zane?" Alaina asked.

He glanced up, startled.

Tony chuckled. "Zane's not really a reader. He's missing out big time, stuck in real life Arcadia Valley."

"Real life's not so bad," put in Cameron. "You all make it sound like there's no value in it, but sometimes a guy's too busy to read, and doesn't need a bunch of fantasies filling his head, anyway." He nodded at Zane. "I feel you, bro."

Zane managed a smile. "Just never got into it."

Kenia grinned, her blue eyes twinkling. "And yet you bid on a gift certificate from Page Turners."

All eyes focused on Zane.

He chuckled, hoping it didn't sound too forced. After all, she knew why he'd done it, and shot him down anyway. "Who knew you didn't sell anything but books?"

Everyone laughed.

A knife screeched against china then a piece of sausage flew off one of the twins' plates, distracting his parents. Only Kenia and Tony stayed looking at Zane.

"I'll buy it from you, man," Tony offered. "I mostly read e-books, but there's this one series with really great cover art that I've been collecting."

"E-books?" asked Kenia in mock horror, pressing her hands to her cheeks. "Say you're kidding me."

Tony grinned at her. "Instant gratification, and easier to pack up when I move."

Right. Tony planned to return to Spokane, so he couldn't be serious about pursuing Kenia, who ran a business here. Kenia wouldn't move away, but the damage might be done.

Aargh. Why couldn't Zane just step up and be a man instead of a bumbling fool when it came to women? He knew. If Kenia got that close, she'd find out his secret. It would matter more to her than most women. Listen to her passion about books. Reading was her life.

The image from the library slid into his mind, of Arthur and that woman bent over a book together. Adult literacy. Was there any chance Arthur could help him?

Maybe the old guy knew a way to tame the words. Maybe there was some secret his teachers hadn't known, some new discovery in the past ten or fifteen years that offered hope.

"Oh, it's you!"

Zane glanced up as a woman loomed over his chair. He stared at her blankly for a moment, trying to place her. Wait. Wasn't she the one he'd shoved that stack of romances at in the Bigby barn?

"I can't thank you enough for your generosity. I didn't even get your name at the benefit, but I've read all five books twice over and just loved them. You really brightened my winter."

Heat crept up Zane's neck and spread over his cheeks. "Uh, you're welcome."

"My little girl wondered why Santa Claus didn't have a white beard and a red suit." She laughed. "I told her he still liked to give gifts even on vacation. Anyway, I have to run, but I couldn't believe my eyes when I saw you over here. I didn't mean to interrupt your time with your friends. Sorry. But I couldn't leave without thanking you again."

He wished she would've. "No problem." He sent mental go-away vibes. After a moment, they seemed to work as she nodded again, gaze sweeping the table, and turned away.

"There's got to be a story in that." Tony looked at him with raised eyebrows.

"Not everything is a story."

"Oh, that's where I think you're wrong. Don't you agree, Kenia? Life is a well-scripted tale. Characters come and characters go. Everything happens for a reason."

Zane glared at his housemate. "Leave it."

Tony lifted both hands. "Sorry, man. You can tell me later."

So not happening. Zane's humiliation was complete without adding that detail. He was only surprised Quinn hadn't told Tony already, though his housemates' schedules rarely crossed.

Maybe it was worth opening up to that Arthur guy. Maybe, just maybe, it was time to start fighting for what he wanted. As it was, his future looked bleak. He might not even have a job come June if he didn't step up his game and, if he took control of that one area, why not more?

The pastor's sermon today had been about reaping what you sowed. He'd quoted a verse about being the person you think you are, deep in your heart, whether positive or negative. He'd made the point that to change the outcome, people had to change from the inside. They couldn't do it alone, but needed to open their hearts to God working in them.

When was the last time Zane had prayed about his inability to read? Maybe he hadn't ever done so. Maybe he'd just accepted that part of himself and buried it deep.

It might not be enough to impress Kenia, but who knew? He'd be seeing her every week at the greenhouse for at least a few months. Tony wouldn't be there, showing off. Zane would be there, taking good care of Clarence.

He wasn't out of the game yet, but, deep inside, the rules were changing. He and God... maybe they could do this.

Chapter 8

*C*LARENCE STOOD AT THE EXIT of the handi-bus, tears moistening his cheeks. Waiting outside the open door, Zane held out his hand, aware of Kenia's presence right behind him. "Come on down, Clarence. You're blocking the exit."

The old man shook himself slightly and descended the few steps, gripping the handrail. "It looks so different."

Didn't the family ever bring him to the place he'd lived his entire life? Probably they were all too busy, though Kenia said she visited her grandfather often. Her parents and brother were probably overloaded running their little empire at the south end of town.

More seniors followed Clarence off Retro Village's bus, looking around in curiosity. Zane maneuvered the wheelchair lift into place for Ida Snyder. Soon a group of the elderly gathered around Kenia.

He'd been avoiding looking at her, trying to keep his

focus on the seniors... and making himself indispensable. But now his gaze settled on her. She wore a bright yellow lightweight jacket that complemented her vibrant orange hair. No doubt she turned heads wherever she went, confident and full of life. Even now she smiled widely at the group surrounding her.

"Hi, everyone. Welcome to the Grace Greenhouse Project. Today we're going to get to know the people who work here and the children who spend time here every day. In fact, I know some of you have great-grandchildren who come to the daycare or the after-school program, right?"

Wilbur Farley nodded and pointed a gnarled hand toward a little girl peering through the wire-mesh fence. "That's my Bethie."

Zane stepped up beside Kenia. "I'm sure she'll be happy to show you around the greenhouse, Wilbur. I know you like cats, and the manager here mentioned that the daycare's cat had kittens a few weeks ago."

Ida looked around her. "Is there a dog? I like dogs better."

"No, ma'am, but Vera is bringing her golden retriever in this evening. Isn't Trixie your favorite?"

"She reminds me of the dog we had years ago."

Zane remembered the stories. "Tanner was a great companion for your kids when they were young." He turned to the group. "So we're going into the play yard now. There's a ramp up to the back deck, and accessible restrooms just inside the door. You're welcome to watch the children play all you want, but for those who are here to get your hands dirty, I'll lead the way into the greenhouse and explain what we'll be doing today."

He was acutely aware of Kenia guiding Ida's wheelchair as they moved into the fenced area. She wasn't just here for Clarence.

She wasn't here for Zane, either. Watching her interact with Tony at Sunday lunch had reminded him of the vast chasm between them.

Young Oliver Kraus dashed to Clarence's side and took his hand. "Come, let me show you the kittens." Clarence sent a longing gaze to the open greenhouse doors as the boy towed him toward a wicker basket nestled just under the back deck.

Zane couldn't micromanage all the residents. Clarence obviously knew the boy. He was an honorary great-grandfather to the twins, or something like that.

"We've got a station set up just inside here," Zane announced. At least, he hoped Alaina had remembered. Yes, there it was. "Come on in, everyone."

A young woman with blond hair in a long ponytail stepped up beside him. "Hi, I'm Cheri, the after-school director. I'm here to help you with the younger half of the participants."

He grinned at her. "Oh, good. Alaina said there'd be someone."

"I'm the one." She rounded up a dozen children and

hollered for Oliver.

In no time, young and old alike crowded around Zane inside the greenhouse, Clarence at the front. Kenia stood at the back of the group with her arm linked through Wilbur's.

"Today we're going to plant some flowers," Zane announced. "There are trays on the tables waiting for potting soil. Then we have a variety of seeds. You can choose a packet for your trays. Once these plants sprout and get well rooted and strong, we'll plant them in some of the flowerbeds over at Retro Village and out along the sidewalk here at the greenhouses."

"Flowers are stinky girl stuff," muttered a young voice. "They make me sneeze."

Zane wasn't sure which boy had said it. "Flowers are pretty. And, hey, when you're old enough to date, you'll find out girls really like getting flowers as a gift, so don't write them off just yet."

The Kraus twins giggled and dug elbows into each other's ribs. Odds were one of them had made the comment. Kenia shifted closer and set her hands on the boys' shoulders, quieting them.

"Next week we'll plant some vegetable seeds, but I thought it would be fun to start with flowers. Any questions?"

Clarence had already shuffled to a nearby table and dumped potting soil into a tray with shaking hands. As much soil missed the tray as landed inside. Oliver ducked away from Kenia's grasp and scrambled over. "Can I help, Granddad?"

Wilbur took his place across from Clarence with Bethie beside him, and Ida pressed the button to move her motorized wheelchair down the gravel path. Two of the other residents hotly debated the merits of marigolds versus pansies. Evan Kraus threw a handful of dirt at a little girl in a white top, but Cheri got to him before Zane could blink.

Zane let out a shaky breath as everyone settled into their tasks. So far so good. A floral scent rose to his nostrils. He didn't even need to look to know Kenia stood beside him, but he couldn't resist a glimpse.

She grinned up at him, laugh lines radiating from her blue eyes, her lips parted. "This is going well."

He pushed out a smile, trying to ignore the increase in his pulse rate. "Yeah, it is." The only way it could be better would be if he dared hope she could ever fall for him. Because, no matter how many times he told himself it was a bad idea, he couldn't help being a bit more attracted to Kenia Akers every time he saw her.

Kenia looked around the busy greenhouse with a satisfied grin. Look at all those eager kids paired up with tottering seniors, being their hands and feet and looking up to the older ones beside them with delight.

Why hadn't she dreamed this up herself? Initially, she'd only thought of getting Granddad's hands in the dirt, but having him here with both his peers and the youngsters was so much better. He thrived on Oliver's attention and let the young boy do most of the work while he scooped his fingers repeatedly through the potting soil.

Although Granddad's voice now lifted querulously above the rest. "Roses don't grow from seeds!"

"Everything grows from seeds. My daddy told me."

Evan was beside his twin in an instant. "Yeah, Dad said even babies grow from seeds."

Uh oh. This didn't seem an appropriate topic for the moment. Kenia hurried closer but collided with Alaina at the corner.

"I've got the boys," mumbled Alaina, her face pink.

That left Kenia with her grandfather. She tugged on his arm, turning him away from the twins. "Don't mind them," she murmured. "What kind of flowers were you and Ollie planting?"

"Marigolds." The disdain in his voice left no question as to his thoughts. "Stinky things but, no, that's what he insisted on."

Kenia laughed. "I love them, odor and all. Wasn't it you who taught me their pheromones ward off pests, keeping the vegetables around them healthier?"

The old man's gaze drifted from her yellow jacket to

her orange hair then back to her eyes. "You look like a marigold."

"I do, don't I? Now you can't tell me they're not pretty, or I'll be hurt. You wouldn't want to pierce your only granddaughter's heart, would you?" She pressed her hand across her chest.

He leaned closer, closing his eyes, and taking a deep whiff.

Uh oh.

"You don't smell like a marigold. More like a lilac." He frowned at her as his voice rose. "It's confusing."

"It's perfume, Granddad."

"But you're allergic. What are you doing here, anyway? Flowers make you sick."

At least he remembered some of it. "Not flowers themselves. Not even all scents, but the chemicals and pesticides on commercial blooms. Coming here where everything is grown organically doesn't make me sick."

"Well, that's convenient," he mumbled.

As though she hadn't *wanted* to work in the flower shop or garden center. She'd been raised to it, same as Grady. Was it her fault the allergies had kicked in, rendering her workdays useless from all the sneezing and itching? Her mother had sure seemed to think so.

Diverting Granddad's attention had worked, but it needed doing again. She could feel curious eyes on her. What did Zane think? He probably already knew. And in any case, it didn't matter. She wasn't dating anyone for a long, long time. She had a broken heart that needed time to mend. Jonah, remember? The guy who couldn't get over loving a married woman enough to fall in love with very available Kenia.

She bit her lip and patted the soil down on the tops of the seed trays. "Where's your helper? You two need to get these watered and plant one more."

"I know what I'm doing," Granddad mumbled then looked around with clouded eyes. "What helper?"

Kenia wasn't sure whether he was serious or not. Sometimes cogs slipped with no warning. She turned as Oliver bounded closer. "Can we plant some red flowers now? That's my new mom's favorite color."

"Roses are red."

Way to come back around, Granddad. "I think there are some dianthus seeds on the rack. And red begonias, too. Let's check them out, Ollie." She held out her hand, but Oliver ignored it and dodged around several of the seniors on his way to the seed packet collection.

She glanced at her watch. Planting time was nearly up. Was Zane prepared for the next part? She looked up to find his eyes focused on her, right where she'd felt them ever since the handi-bus had pulled in.

"Children!" called Cheri a few minutes later. "It's story time. Please wash up and gather in the story nook."

Zane's jaw firmed and twitched slightly as his gaze slid away from Kenia. Strange reaction, unless he were purposefully breaking the visual connection. Had she been staring at him? She didn't think so.

No, she couldn't read too much into it. Not with the kids pouring through the greenhouse doors and up the ramp to the center. Her job was the older folks. Granddad? But he was hurrying nearly as much as the young ones, swept along in their tide. Maybe Ida needed a hand.

Kenia walked beside the motorized wheelchair as it rolled up the ramp and into the bright, cheery space with its murals of children playing, reading, and playing games amid stalks of giant flowers. Evelyn had hired Cheri to paint the imaginative space then kept her on when she discovered the single mom was as good at wrangling kids as painting them. Definitely a win for the project as a whole.

The phone rang, and Alaina excused herself to her office and shut the door. The kids wrestled on the rug as Cheri settled onto a low seat in the corner and picked up a hardcover.

Kenia recognized the book as one she'd recommended and ordered for the daycare. So many great titles existed now that encouraged children's love of the outdoors and tending gardens.

"What's this, eh?" Granddad mumbled, staring around him. "This is my living room, but where's my chair?"

This might be the first time he'd been inside since the renovation had been completed. Kenia mentally chided herself for not thinking how it would affect him. She edged around the group and reached for his arm. "Granddad."

He stared at her, confusion clouding his vision. "Eleanor?"

Her grandmother's name. The grandmother she barely remembered, since she'd passed away when Kenia was a kid no older than the ones in this room. Dad sometimes mentioned that Kenia reminded him of his mother, but her grandfather had never looked at her like this before.

Kenia rubbed her hand up and down his arm. "It's okay, Granddad. Eleanor's gone, remember?"

His jaw trembled as his eyes glistened. "I miss her."

Her heart clenched. "I know you do." How much longer would the family have him in their life?

Cheri began the story. "Once upon a time, two children named —"

Oliver screamed.

Kenia whirled back to the group, her hand still on Granddad's arm, to see Evan staring in shock at Oliver with blood spurting from his nose. She started toward him, but Cheri was quicker.

"Evan, time out." Cheri thrust the book at Zane as she surged to her feet. "You read. I've got Oliver."

Evan backed away, eyes wide and hands over his mouth while Cheri scooped Oliver and headed for the restroom.

Granddad wobbled. "Blood."

Kenia put her arm around his waist, hoping he wouldn't take a tumble himself at the sight. She glanced over at Zane who stood at the front of the now-quiet assembly staring at the book in his hand as though it were a rattler.

What was all that about?

Chapter 9

ANE FROZE. HOW, WITH ALL the adults that had been in the room seconds before, had he been the one left holding the book? Young children sat cross-legged on the rug, faces expectantly peering up at him. Behind them, the residents sat on chairs or stood at the back, no less expectant. Kenia, her arms wrapped around her grandfather's thin waist, held the old man upright but, she, too, was focused on Zane.

He glanced at the book, with its cover illustration of a child peering at a plant through a magnifying glass. Words writhed around the image. He couldn't read this. Not only because of his panic, but because the letters danced with glee as though daring him to catch them.

He couldn't.

His gaze collided with Kenia's and held. Her head tilted slightly as her eyebrows rose. Zane held out the book to her, a tiny gesture, but one she seemed to understand. Or maybe it was the desperate pleading and panic in his eyes.

Kenia steered Clarence to a chair and settled him then wended between the children and took the book from Zane's hand before sitting on the low stool Cheri had vacated. She opened the book, holding it with the pictures facing the audience, and began to read with expression.

How did she do that? She only glanced at the pages... from upside down, no less. And yet the story made sense and was even kind of cute as the fictional children learned about the flowers.

Longing grew in Zane as he stared at the illustrated pictures. *Why, God? Why can't I do that? It seems so easy when other people do it.*

He heard the reply, nearly audibly. *You can do all things through Him who gives you strength.*

It wasn't a case of muscle, though. It wasn't a case of mind over matter. If it were, he would have mastered this thing a long time ago. He wanted it. He yearned for it.

Enough to humble yourself and ask for help?

Pride. Was that all that stood in his way? It couldn't be. All those other people couldn't be faking their ability to read. Tony and Kenia talked about books they'd both read. The words had meant the same thing to both of them, just like in high school English class when they'd discussed *The Great Gatsby*. The class nerds had dug through worn paperbacks to dispute

Valerie Comer

passages Zane only recalled from the movie.

The memory of the older man and the middle-aged woman leaning over that book together in the library window seemed as clear as the children in front of him. He'd give it one last try. He'd ask for Arthur like the poster said and humiliate himself by admitting he was a grown man who couldn't read. He'd explain about the letters and words undulating on the page, and the kind-looking man would try to hide his smile at Zane's vivid imagination.

No. He had to stop thinking like that. Sure, God had made him unique, but could he really be the only person on the planet to whom this happened? Was he *that* special? If so, it was time he knew it for sure. And if he wasn't, maybe somebody could help him corral the words. If others could do it, so could he. This time, he wouldn't let pride interfere.

Now if only Kenia wouldn't corner him about what happened... but was that pride talking again? Of all the people he didn't want to tell, she was at the top of his list. A beautiful woman with a sparkling smile. And a bookstore.

❧

Kenia curled up in the easy chair and accepted the cup of tea from her sister-in-law, Joanna.

"I was sorry to hear about your breakup with Jonah

Baxter," Joanna said, settling in across from her.

"Ancient history." Kenia waved a hand. "That happened a month ago."

"But still, I'm sure it hurt to find out he was in love with someone else. A married woman at that."

"That's his problem, not mine." Not anymore. "Besides, Gloria's been separated from her husband for years and hadn't even told anyone she'd been married. It wasn't Jonah's fault."

Joanna's eyebrows rose. "No regrets?"

"Some, I guess." The swirling tea captured all of Kenia's attention. "Who doesn't want their own happily-ever-after? You found yours — hard to believe anyone would want my big brother, but there you go."

The other woman laughed softly. "Sometimes love captures you when you're not even looking for it. I'd come to Arcadia Valley to get away from a bad situation with my ex-boyfriend and to help my brother out with the twins. I was nursing my wounds and as prickly as a porcupine."

Kenia remembered. Not that she'd hung out with Grady all that much back then. He was five years older and completely immersed in the garden center. In fact, she could be thankful Joanna had provided a link between them so they were now closer than ever.

Joanna eyed her over the cup of tea. "You seemed to hit it off with Tony Santoro that Sunday we all went out for lunch. He's new in town, young, single, a Christian."

She snapped her fingers, eyes dancing with mirth. "And, oh, he can cook. That's a bonus."

"I'm going to take cooking lessons." She'd just decided, two seconds ago.

"Tony was one of our teachers at the class Grady and I took last fall."

"*Different* lessons."

Her sister-in-law chuckled. "Oh, you're funny. Why not him? He's such an avid reader, too. I can't think of a single what's-not-to-like about him."

Valid question, really. She ought to be attracted to the guy, not his brooding housemate who hadn't entered the conversation. Who'd wordlessly begged her to read the children's story the other day at Grace, like the book was burning his fingers. Who'd apparently given away the stack of hardbacks he'd bid on and won at Allie Bigby's benefit concert.

Why would a guy who seemed allergic to books be more attractive than Tony Santoro?

"Or maybe his friend. Wasn't his name Zane? Pretty quiet, though."

"Not when you're one-on-one. He's interesting. Funny."

Joanna's eyebrows peaked. "So that's the way the wind blows."

"I'm not sure." Should she ask her sister-in-law's opinions? "He's intriguing, but I don't know what to make of him. I'll be working with him at the greenhouse when he brings Granddad and the others by for their weekly visit. Granddad likes him."

Joanna scrunched her face. "That's a bonus. He still calls me Vanity sometimes."

Kenia laughed. "At least I don't have an indiscretion like Grady's, having been engaged to Vanessa when Granddad couldn't stand her." No, her reputation was clean. No one had come close to capturing her heart until Jonah, but even that hadn't been love. She could see it now.

Now that Zane Russell's dark eyes, deep dimple, and too-long hair had captured her imagination.

"So that's great," Joanna said. "You'll get to know him and see what happens. Have you told your parents?"

"No, and don't you dare drop any hints. There's nothing to tell." Mom and Dad had told everyone they knew about her relationship with Jonah. They'd been so proud of her prospects and wanted the world to know. Mom was choked she'd broken it off and was barely speaking to her. Apparently Kenia should have tried harder and won Jonah over.

Joanna lifted a hand. "You've got it. Just don't plan your wedding for September, okay?"

"Sept—"

A warm blush rose on her sister-in-law's face.

Kenia squealed. "Are you pregnant?"

Joanna nodded, a small smile lifting her lips.

"Oh, I'm so excited! Have you told Mom and Dad they're going to be grandparents?"

"Not yet, and please don't tell anyone until we announce it." Her eyes twinkled. "You keep our secret, and I'll keep yours."

"Blackmail..." breathed Kenia. "I have a question for you. The real reason I came, that is."

"Not just to have tea and share secrets?"

"Not just." But she really ought to make more of an effort to hang out with her sister-in-law, especially now that Joanna was no longer trying to set any available woman up with Cameron. Nope, Kenia's housemate had snagged Joanna's brother and married him at Christmas.

She pulled in a deep breath. "I'm sure you know Aunt Irene wants to retire, just like Dad and Mom do."

"Right."

"We've talked for a couple of years about me buying the bookstore from her. Max Martinez has given her a quote for what he thinks she could get on the open market, and she's offered me a good deal quite a bit lower."

"That's great. You're going to do it, aren't you?"

"Yeah, I plan to. I mean, it's what I've been working toward since my allergies got too bad to continue at the flower shop. I've got options few women under thirty have."

Joanna nodded. "But..."

"She gave me options. Buying only the business, or

buying the building as well."

"Oooh!"

"I know. I've always pestered her to open the two halves to each other and expand the bookstore, but she wasn't sure Arcadia Valley was big enough to make it worthwhile."

"The other half is empty now, isn't it?"

"Yes, that's part of what makes it tempting. If I bought the building, Aunt Irene would move out of the apartment upstairs and leave it for me, so I'd save money on rent. The apartment is bigger than my cottage out by El Corazon."

"It's a nice space. Airy."

"Yes. It could use a coat of paint to freshen it up, but it's not bad."

"Would Irene keep the building if you decided to only buy Page Turners?"

"That's the thing." Kenia shook her head, sucking in her lip. "She'd list the building with Max."

"And it's possible that whoever purchased it would want the whole thing, and the bookstore would no longer have a home."

"You nailed it in one."

"So why not just buy it? If you need a loan, I'm sure your parents would help you out. Have you asked them?"

"Mom's still annoyed with me for breaking up with Jonah."

Joanna rolled her eyes. "Give her something else to think about."

"Maybe *you* should."

"Don't throw Grady and me under the bus. We have our reasons for waiting a few more weeks to make our announcement."

Kenia sighed. "I'm sure Irene and Dad have talked about it already."

"Then your parents are probably just waiting for you to bring up the subject."

Her sister-in-law was probably right.

"Unless you're having second thoughts about being tied to a bookstore for the rest of your life."

Kenia bit her lip. "Not full-on second thoughts, but kind of."

"Tell me."

"I guess... I don't want to turn into Irene. I don't want to spend my entire life alone, wrapped up in that bookstore."

"She was married once."

"Yeah, Uncle Gerald died in an accident when they were newlyweds."

"And she never married again."

Kenia shook her head. "She poured all her energy, her focus — everything — into Page Turners."

"Maybe she wanted it that way."

"Maybe, but I don't. I want a husband, kids, a life outside of work. I'm afraid owning a business will suck everything else away."

"It doesn't have to. You can hire staff so you can have more time. Countless women have made having a family and a retail outlet work."

"Will you keep working after the baby?"

Joanna shrugged. "Having my own consulting business does make it easier. I can take on fewer clients for a while. I've already turned down one big project near Boise I just don't have the energy to deal with."

Kenia leaned back in the armchair and eyed her sister-in-law. "You're a real estate consultant. What would you advise me to do? For free, of course."

"I don't give advice for free." Joanna laughed and winked. "Pray about it. Like, really pray. You don't have to buy any of it at all. You can say no to your aunt and look for a different job, or start a different kind of venture completely. You took business management at the University of Utah, didn't you?"

"I did." But... a whole different life that didn't revolve around the flower shop or the bookstore? It hardly seemed possible.

"You could go into business with Grady and work with him at the garden center." Joanna held up a hand. "Yes, I know about your allergies, but he's working toward more organics. You could leave Bryanna Kujak in charge of the flower shop and help oversee the business at a higher level. From an off-site office, even."

"I gave that up, years ago."

"I know. But this is a time to examine all your options, not just whether to buy the building or only the business. Make sure you're following your own dreams, not your parents' dreams or your aunt's dreams. If you could do anything you wanted — anything at all — what would your life look like?"

Anything at all? Zane grinned at her with that lopsided grin, a baby in his arms.

Okay, this wasn't a dream. More like a hallucination. But what if it could be true? She scrunched her eyes shut and let it play out. They lived in the upstairs apartment with their children, dark haired like their daddy. It had three bedrooms, after all. Downstairs, the bookstore spilled into a coffee bar, maybe with a used book section beside a fireplace. Maybe an outlet for local crafts, like Serena's pottery and Allie's lavender salves. Maybe a space for a book club or hopeful writers to meet.

She searched for a different dream. One that took place away from the familiar tall shelving units loaded with the sweet aroma of ink on fresh paper. One without readers like Perlita Ricci waiting eagerly for the newest volume in their favorite series.

Maybe the bookstore was her dream, after all.

"I'll pray with you," Joanna offered then chuckled. "And maybe find a way to set you up with Zane Russell."

"I'll take the prayers, but you start meddling with my love life, and I'll tell the world you're pregnant."

Chapter 10

*J*S... IS ARTHUR IN?" Zane shifted from one foot to the other in front of the library desk. The nearest shelving units seemed to lean toward him, threatening to tip and send an avalanche of books to crush him. No. He took a deep breath. They were at least ten feet away.

Charlotte Delis looked up and swept long hair over her shoulder. "Arthur?"

"The guy from the poster." Zane thumbed over his shoulder. "I want to talk to him."

The librarian's gaze slid past him then back to his eyes with a faintly perplexed expression. "He's a volunteer, so he's not here all the time. His number is on the poster, if you want to give him a call."

That all-too-familiar flush crept up Zane's neck. Why had he assumed the number would be the library's and he could sidestep plugging it into his phone? He should have tried harder to decipher the poster. The way he's misread the program name taunted him. Lite racy. Talk about stupid.

"Or you can leave a message, and I can get him to call you."

Relief rolled over him. "I'd appreciate that."

Charlotte pulled a notebook closer, picked up a pen, and looked up at him.

"Zane Russell."

"Oh, I remember you. You picked up all the gardening books for your children. How did they like them? Will you be starting a garden this spring?"

"I. Uh." His new way to do things was to tell the truth and not let people assume things about him. "I don't actually have a family. The books were for a program we're running with Retro Village over at the Grace Greenhouse, getting the residents and the kids gardening together."

Her face lit up. "What a lovely idea! I've heard such good things about all the programs at Grace. My daughter, Elena — well, my stepdaughter — begged her dad and me to volunteer at the gardens there, growing food for the soup kitchen. It's wonderful to see the town rally together like that."

No comment about the little white lie when he'd let her assume the books were for his children? His conscience nudged. Not just assume. He'd told her the kids were younger. Not only because the kids in the program were younger, but because he'd needed books he could read himself. If there were only a few large words on a page, he could block them off and decipher them.

He'd learned more from YouTube, though. A lot more.

"It's a great venture, and the residents are delighted to be part of it. Plus, they love spending time with the kids. Seems to be mutual."

Charlotte's grin widened. "Giving the generations opportunities to interact is a blessing for everyone." She tapped the pen lightly. "What's your message for Arthur?"

Here it came. Instead of the bright smile, her lips would frown in disdain. It didn't matter. She was a married woman with a child. Only Kenia's opinion mattered, and even that wasn't enough to hold him back anymore. He had to do this for himself. If it lost him any chance with Kenia Akers, well, he didn't have much of one anyway. "I think that poster is about him teaching people to read. I could use some help."

If her expression flickered, it was only for an instant. "That's Arthur's passion. I know he'd love to get together with you. How can he contact you?"

Zane rattled off his phone number then gave his work hours as unavailable times. He watched as Charlotte wrote down the information in neat rows. Then the parts began to jiggle. "Do you... do you think he can help me?"

She looked up. "I know he can."

"How can you be sure?"

"Everyone who wants to read can be helped. Besides, Arthur knows what it's like. He told me he has Scotopic Sensitivity Syndrome, which basically means that pages of text wouldn't hold still for him. He did poorly in school because his teachers thought he was just laz—"

"Words jitter." Zane stared at her as he gripped the edge of the desk. "They spiral in circles. They trip over each other and vanish if you stare at them."

"That sounds like Arthur's descriptions." Charlotte pulled a book out of a stack on her desk and opened it, turning it toward him. "Tell me what you see."

Besides a solid wall of tiny print? Oh, wait. "There are white rivers running from the top to the bottom." His finger traced one of them. "No, they're gone. Now they're all just a jumble. Letters stacked on top of letters."

"Let me give Arthur a call and see if he's free right now."

"No, it's okay. I don't want to be a bother."

Charlotte pointed one finger at him while the other hand reached for the phone on her desk. "Not a bother, Zane. Not at all. He's going to be so excited to meet with you."

Zane couldn't help the frown that pulled his brows together. Now he was going to perform like a monkey in a circus? Provide entertainment for all? Great. Just what he needed. He backed up. "No. Don't worry about it. I have somewhere I need to be."

But he didn't. Not for a couple of hours. Hadn't he braced himself, convinced himself it was time to face up to his issues and seek help? But there wasn't help, even if Charlotte said there was. Even if Arthur had some sort of syndrome. Zane didn't want a pity party. Didn't want to be a lab rat. Didn't want these bookcases tilting in on him.

He fled into the March drizzle.

Zane had sure been acting strange for the past week or two. Maybe Kenia had been reading too much into the way his gaze had lingered on hers. She'd thought he'd ask her out again, like he had the day soon after Valentine's when he'd come into Page Turners clutching his gift certificate. She'd say yes this time, but he didn't come. There'd been flickers of what seemed to be interest, but now, nothing.

He worked with the seniors and the children on Tuesday afternoons, came to church on Sundays with Tony, but didn't even glance her way. Barely acknowledged or responded to a direct question.

Why had she wasted a single daydream on this exasperating man? Even now he leaned against the far wall, arms crossed over his chest as he watched Cheri reading a story. As the two groups had gotten to know each other, more kids nestled next to their favorite seniors for story time. The program was a success.

Zane glanced over and their gazes collided for one brief second. Then he turned back to Cheri, his expression never changing.

Attraction? What attraction? She'd imagined it all, just like she had with Jonah. No, that wasn't quite true. Jonah had been impulsive. He'd invited her to be his date to his brother's wedding the second time they'd talked one on one, just after Christmas. They'd danced at the wedding and kissed to welcome the New Year. She'd had high hopes he might be her husband before the year was out, but those hopes had been dashed.

Kenia was the common denominator. Ben Kujak and Cameron Kraus had never spared her a glance, not that she'd wanted them to. Jonah couldn't fall in love with her. Tony was fun to talk to, but there wasn't any spark there. Now Zane seemed determined to avoid her. What, did she have cooties or something?

And if she bought her aunt's bookstore, wouldn't that scare men off even more? The image of a professional businesswoman. Independent. Nerdy.

She glanced at Zane again. This time he crouched beside Ida Snyder's wheelchair and offered the senior a warm smile as she whispered in his ear.

The chill was only for her.

Cheri closed the book.

"Another story!" called Ophelia Poncetta.

"I'm sorry, but the handi-bus is waiting to take our friends back to Retro Village. It's time to say goodbye to them until next week."

Kenia linked her arm with Granddad's as he heaved to his feet. Oliver, Evan, and a couple of other kids crushed his middle with hugs before she walked him outside, where Zane stood waiting to help each senior onto the bus.

"Thanks, Zane," she said softly as he took Granddad's arm.

He nodded without meeting her gaze. "Here you go, Clarence."

Kenia turned away, back into the children's center, as tears blurred her eyes. Maybe instead of buying Page Turners, she should leave town. Not because of Zane, exactly, but to give herself a fresh start where everyone didn't already know her as the geeky girl who couldn't catch a guy to save her life. She had to give Aunt Irene an answer soon, by the end of the month.

Alaina grabbed her arm when she re-entered the main room. "Did you hear about Gloria?"

Kenia took a deep breath. Did she look like she *wanted* to be updated on the gossip?

"Her ex divorced her back in January. He was in town and served her the papers himself."

In January? Two months ago? "Now that's convenient."

Alaina's brows pulled together. "What do you mean?"

"Jonah could at least have been polite enough to tell me instead of leading me on for a couple of more weeks before I figured out we had no future."

"That's the thing." Her friend leaned closer. "He didn't know. It didn't come out publicly until just a day or two ago. I heard Jonah was just as surprised as anyone else."

"Are you kidding me? Why on earth would Gloria have kept that secret to herself?" Kenia stared at Alaina. "Please don't tell me she's still in love with *Frank*?" Talk about confusing. Gloria in love with Frank. Jonah in love with Gloria. Kenia in love with Jonah... or so she'd imagined a couple of months ago.

Alaina shook her head. "No, I don't think so. She just didn't feel free."

"I keep hearing that, but it doesn't make sense."

"Cameron and I talked about it. Lisa is the one who left him, you know. She sent the divorce papers, so he didn't have to make that decision. He's not sure how long it would have taken for him to make the move himself instead of hoping she'd come back." Alaina scrunched up her face. "Not that they'd had anything good going on for a long time before she left. Divorce doesn't tend to happen in a vacuum."

Kenia heaved a big sigh. "I'm sure it doesn't."

"The thing is, Cameron signed to protect the twins. If he'd waited, would Lisa have come to her senses and realized she was leaving the best part of herself behind? I don't mean Cameron so much — although I think he's pretty awesome — but the twins. I love those boys so much, Kenia. I just don't know how she could walk away from them."

"But Gloria and Frank didn't have kids. Although who knows, right? She hasn't exactly been upfront about things."

"No, they didn't have kids. You're right. Things might've been different then."

Maybe. Maybe not. Nothing the police officer did made any sense to Kenia. The woman had been separated from Frank for nearly a decade. She could have just divorced the guy and embraced her happily-ever-after with Jonah forever ago. Doves, rainbows, and glitter. Not that Gloria was the glitter kind, exactly. But, still, why purposefully kill her chances?

"Well, congrats to her and Jonah then. I imagine wedding bells are just around the corner." Kenia ought to be happy for them. Really.

Alaina shook her head. "I don't think they're actually dating, at least not yet."

"That doesn't even make sense. Why would she have waited to tell him? I respect her for not horning in while he and I were going out, but that's been history for more than a month. She's had lots of time to make her move... if she loves him, that is."

"I guess life isn't as simple as we like to think."

Kenia leaned closer. "But it is. If we don't go after what we want, nothing will ever happen. Who wants to die an old lady with a pile of regrets? Not me."

"So, what do you want? What are you going after?"

Did she look like some kind of loser? Just because she'd been unlucky with men the past few years didn't mean the right guy wasn't out there. She'd been waiting on Zane to make the next move — again — but maybe it was up to her. After all, he'd asked her out once, and she'd turned him down. The ball was in her court. She'd get to the bottom of whatever his problem was, they'd solve it together, and then the doves and rainbows would be hers.

She'd take the glitter, too.

Chapter 11

WHAT'S UP, MAN? You've been grouchy as a bear wakened early from his winter nap for ages now."

Zane stared at Tony. Had he really been that bad? Yeah. Yeah, he had.

Tony tapped a button and the tablet screen blacked out. "Talk to me."

"Got things on my mind."

"I figured. Sometimes it's good to share them with someone. Maybe we can bounce ideas. Or I can pray for you more intelligently at least."

"You pray for me?"

Tony shrugged. "Sure, I do. And more than the 'God bless Mommy and Daddy and Zane' verbiage of my childhood."

"Well, thanks. I appreciate it."

"If you'd rather help me cook supper while we talk,

I'm good with that." Tony flipped his tablet back on, navigated to a different screen, and shoved it at Zane. "How does this sound?"

Zane stared at the photo of pasta, tomatoes, and green leaves. This was his opportunity. *Lord, help me.* He pushed the tablet back. "I can't read that."

"Can't?" Tony's voice was quiet.

Zane dared a glance at his housemate, who sat patiently waiting, face impassive. "Can't."

"How did you..."

"Get through school? I didn't." Now that he'd uttered his secret, the words kept coming. "It's not that I don't know the letters or the sounds they make. It's that they don't hold still."

"I wondered."

"Well, now you know. I'm a loser." Wait, he'd promised himself he was done talking about himself like that.

"Definitely not." Tony pulled to his feet and entered the kitchen. "I'd say it takes a lot of courage to do so well in a world that revolves around the written word."

"Do so well?" Zane laughed. "What kind of *doing well* do you see around here?"

"I see a guy who owns his own home—"

"Inherited from my grandparents."

"Who's done a lot of work to it."

"Nothing complicated."

Tony's eyebrows rose. "You took out a load-bearing

wall and put in an arch to the living room. The finish work in here is impeccable."

"I got Drew Harrison's advice. It wasn't hard."

"Who's got a good job. Who—"

Zane held up his hand. "I can't even count the jobs I've lost or never had a chance at because of being unable to read. Because of not having my high school diploma. Don't try to make me feel better, Santoro. It's not working."

Tony opened the fridge and took out a package of chicken breasts. "Want to chunk those up and give them some salt and pepper?"

"Sure."

"Low carb is hitting Italian cuisine, so we're going to try this tonight with zucchini noodles."

Zane raised his eyebrows at Tony. "Seriously?"

"They're a thing." Tony grinned. "They're called zoodles."

"You've got to be kidding me. What's wrong with fettuccine?"

"I told you. Carbohydrates. Lots of people are going with a ketogenic diet, avoiding stuff made with wheat flour, sugar, stuff like that."

"Bread?"

Tony sliced his hand through the air. "Gone."

Zane winced. "Spare me."

"Me, too. But a chef needs to be watching trends, adapting yesterday's favorites to today's palates." Tony pointed at a paper bag on the counter. "Don't panic. I picked up a loaf of sourdough from A Slice of Heaven this morning."

"Whew." Zane pulled a cutting board from the cupboard, dumped the chicken on it, and began to slice.

"Thing is, most jobs today require some reading. Cooking, too."

"Tell me about it."

"But there's ways to get better at it. I think the library has a program."

"They do."

Tony pulled two large zucchinis out of the fridge and glanced over. "You give it a try?"

"I looked into it." Arthur had left a couple of voicemails, but Zane hadn't returned his calls.

"What have you got to lose?"

Pride? Zane sighed. "You're right. I've spent my entire life hiding it. Pretending it didn't matter, but it does."

"Why now?"

Kenia. But it wasn't just her. He was just so tired of being on the sidelines. Of never feeling like he was good enough for an intelligent woman, for a good job, for life. He shrugged and ground black pepper and Himalayan salt over the chicken.

"Kenia Akers runs a bookstore," Tony said casually.

"Makes her perfect for *you*, don't you think? Imagine getting all the books you want at cost."

"She despises my e-reader addiction." Tony chuckled. "And besides, it's not me she keeps an eye on. It's you."

"As if."

"Bro. Are you blind or just stupid?"

Knife poised, Zane narrowed his gaze at his housemate.

Tony held both hands in the air. "I'm not talking about reading. I mean about women."

"And you're the expert?"

"Nah, not pretending that. I've been on the move too much the past few years. Too immersed in my career to think about a relationship. When I get to Spokane, I'll be crazy busy starting my own restaurant. It'll make the hours I've put in so far look like child's play. It's going to be a while before I have time to think about dating." He peered at the chicken. "Mind sautéing that up?"

"Sure." Tony was right. Zane was as settled as he was likely to get, unless he got a job somewhere else and sold the house. He didn't really want to. He'd always loved visiting Arcadia Valley in years gone by, and he was in no hurry to move away. And for what?

His roommate turned the zucchini into noodle-like strands with a small machine while Zane shoved chicken around a frying pan.

"So, about reading."

Should've known the guy wouldn't leave it. "What about it?"

"Why not get some help? Other people have learned to read as adults. You can, too."

"You don't understand. It's not easy for me like it is for you. How do you make the words stand still?"

Tony turned toward him, eyebrows pulled together. "What do you mean, stand still?"

"They ripple. Don't tell me you haven't noticed. All I want to know is how you tame them."

"Ripple?"

Zane stared at him and made a waving motion with his hand.

"Words don't move."

"They do for me."

Tony looked thoughtful, not laughing as Zane had half-expected. "I read an article about that once."

Zane snorted. "Of course, you did."

"Seriously. There are things they can do for that."

"Right."

"Bro, you are not alone, and there's help out there. Talk to the guy at the literacy program and, if he can't help, I'll do some digging online. We'll figure it out."

Against his better judgment, Zane felt a twinge of rising hope. Tony wouldn't steer him wrong just to get a laugh at his expense, would he?

"I'll finish up making the caprese pollo while you call the guy, okay?" Tony dumped the zucchini noodles into a sauté pan. "You've got about ten minutes."

Zane tugged his phone out of his hip pocket. "You're

sure? This is real?"

"So real, man. Do it."

He navigated to the phone icon and tapped the number in his recents.

"Arthur Smythe here. How can I help you?"

Zane turned aside out of the kitchen. "This is Zane Russell calling."

Kenia arranged the display table with a range of yellow and purple book covers surrounding the bouquet of daffodils she'd picked from the long border at Grace Greenhouse. They were more casually arranged than something from her mom's shop, but they also didn't make her sneeze.

There. That brought a bit of much-needed spring sunshine into Page Turners. The shop didn't get a lot of direct sunlight, which was probably a good thing for the merchandise, but Kenia missed it. The other half of the building, though, sided on Washington Street. Maybe a window or two could be punched through the brick façade when she renovated. It looked like some had once existed.

Was she really going to do this? Her parents thought it was a great idea. Dad had poured over his sister's bank statements and figured there was room for growth, especially if Kenia diversified. She had an appointment with Denise Marshall at Wells Fargo Bank down the street tomorrow morning.

If she kept focused on the store, she wouldn't think about how she'd tried to get Zane aside a few days ago at the greenhouse, but never somehow managed. How was she supposed to talk to him when he was constantly bent over Ida Snyder or Wilbur Farley? She did have his email address — she'd used it to send him the proposal over a month ago — but if he was avoiding her in person, ignoring an email would be a piece of cake.

The bells tinkled as the door opened, and Kenia turned to greet her customer.

Jonah? An aroma of warm chocolate chip cookies swirled from the box in his hands.

"Hey, Kenia." He offered a lopsided smile.

She took a step back. "Hi." He couldn't possibly be here with a peace offering. How could he have fallen out of love with Gloria when rumor had it they'd actually gone on a date or two? Not after all this. Not when Kenia was moving on, or, at least, trying to.

"I wanted to come by and tell you how sorry I am."

What, had someone died she didn't know about? Kenia crossed her arms over her chest. "For...?"

He shook his head. "I wasn't playing fair with you this winter. Trying to convince you and me both that my heart was free. It was a mistake, and I hate that you suffered for it." He held out the box. "Truce?"

Kenia sighed. "I knew all along, at least to some

degree. It wasn't your fault, not really. I convinced myself that a slow start was a good thing, that we were getting to know each other as friends first, and the passion would follow." Had she really just said that word to Jonah? Oh, man.

"Me, too. I like you a lot, Kenia. We had some good times together."

She studied his face.

"I'm thankful—now—that you broke up with me when you did. I deserved it, and we're both happier now. Or at least I hope you are."

"So it all worked out with Gloria?"

Jonah nodded. "I think so, anyway. I'm working two jobs right now, at the bakery and running L'Aubergine while Morgan is recovering from breast cancer surgery. Did you know about that?"

"I was sorry to hear. I hope she'll be okay."

"They think they got everything so, yeah. I hope so, too. Anyway, I haven't been able to spend much time with Gloria with everything that's going on. Probably a good thing, since her divorce is so recent. She needs time to process it."

"Jonah? She's been over Frank for like eight years."

"Well, yes, but still. And I worried what you'd think, too. I mean, we were dating not so long ago."

Kenia rolled her eyes. "Seriously, Jonah. Stop overthinking things. Everyone in Arcadia Valley except you and me knew you were in love with Gloria the whole time. We knew it, too, but we were trying to ignore it. So move on already."

"Only if you take these cookies off my hands."

"Fine. Twist my arm with fresh cookies." She chuckled. "I'll take them if I have to."

He grinned as she accepted the box. "I was wondering if you had the newest book in that series I've been collecting in stock?"

"Now I know the real reason you felt the need to apologize. You only loved me for my books." Hopefully her smile would remove the sting from her words.

"Not only, but I'm tired of shopping in Twin Falls, that's for sure. You've got a much better selection in fantasy."

She eyed him. "I'm thinking of buying my aunt out. Expanding into the storefront next door. Maybe adding a coffee bar and selling the work of some local artisans."

"Good idea. My sister-in-law would probably be all over that. She was talking about looking for a retailer downtown who might want to handle her pottery." He nodded thoughtfully as he looked around. "I'm sure you'll do really well at whatever you choose, Kenia. You're a smart woman. Smart enough to turn a guy like me loose." He yawned.

"What hours are you working at L'Aubergine, anyway? Are you getting enough sleep?"

"Too many, and no. I was on my way back to the farmhouse for a nap between the two kitchens, but I told

Micah I needed to see you first. I'm glad I came by." He poked his chin toward the box. "Enjoy the cookies, and let me know when the book comes in."

"Will do."

He turned toward the door then looked back. "Oh, I meant to tell you. Ruth and Corban expect to bring the baby home this weekend. I think the little guy will be okay."

"I'm glad to hear that." And she was, even though Jonah's sister had always been a little aloof with Kenia. Ruth had seen what they'd refused to see: they would never be family.

Kenia tucked the box of cookies under the counter. Okay, she'd have one — just one — now, while they were so fresh. The door to Jonah had not only been shut but officially locked. Bolted. Key tossed into Arcadia Creek.

Chocolate chips melted on her tongue. They tasted like freedom, like helium balloons released to the breeze. Like the future. Had she needed this bit of closure as much as Jonah had? It seemed so.

Chapter 12

PASTOR IVAN SURVEYED THE congregation on Sunday morning. "Some of you may have already heard about the shooting in our little town on Friday. I know the prayer chain was notified to send a prayer request for our sister in Christ, Gloria Sinclair, one of our police officers. Gloria was shot in the shoulder and lost a lot of blood before they got her into surgery. She's out of danger now and thanks you for your continued prayers." He glanced at his notes on the podium then looked up with a smug grin. "Oh, and they caught the guy who shot her."

Wow. Zane shifted in his pew. He'd never expected to hear of anything like this happening in Arcadia Valley. It always seemed the epitome of a sleepy, safe, small town.

"The Bible says in Galatians that we reap what we sow. The question is, how specific is that? How personal? Did Officer Sinclair deserve to be shot because of a past action on her part? In other words, do we always get what we deserve?"

Zane hoped not. If he got what he deserved, there'd be hell to pay. Literally.

"Let's have a look at the book of Job today. You probably recall the gist of the story but, if you're a typical believer, you've skimmed those forty-two chapters a couple of times in your life and called it a win. It's hard to make sense of, but let's take a few minutes this morning for an overview. Job lived in early biblical days, probably long before Moses. He was a wealthy man who had ten children and many flocks and herds. Above all, he was a righteous man with no equal."

Pastor Ivan paused and looked around the gathering. "If anyone deserved to reap a long, happy, healthy life, it was Job. But that's not what happened. In a turn of events we don't really understand, Satan came before God and accused God of protecting Job. He basically said that if Job didn't feel so blessed, he'd turn his back on God and curse Him. But God figured Job was up for the challenge."

Zane had met a challenge or two in his life. He'd heard of Job and knew his own circumstances had nothing on the patriarch. But, unlike Job, he'd accused God of abandoning him.

"With God's permission, Satan hit Job with everything he had. Have a look at the first chapter. Job lost everything. His family died. His herds and flocks were killed or stolen. He had nothing left, but still penned the famous words, 'Naked I came from my mother's womb, and naked I will depart. The Lord gave and the Lord has taken away; may the name of the Lord be praised.' Satan was annoyed with that response. He said God was still protecting the man, and God accepted the challenge on Job's behalf and allowed further testing. This time Satan attacked Job's body and covered him with painful boils. Even when his wife urged him to curse God and die, Job did not sin in what he said. His response? 'Shall we accept good from God, and not trouble?'"

Ouch. How many times had Zane blamed God for the little things that went wrong? Compared to the patriarch, Zane's struggle with reading was of no importance. He'd lost a relationship with his parents because of it. He'd lost his grandparents due only to old age. He hadn't lost everything, and he certainly didn't have pain from head to toe.

"So here's the thing," Pastor Ivan went on. "While it is generally true that we reap what we sow, even the Bible teaches it's an overly simplistic saying. Job's friends considered his problems as punishment from a just God for a secret sin. Eliphaz says, 'as I have observed, those who plow evil and those who sow trouble reap it.' Isn't that our struggle, too, as we try to make sense of the evil in this world?"

The police officer hadn't deserved to be shot, Zane was pretty sure. She was a cop, doing what cops did, and the perp had done what bad guys did. Officer Sinclair was simply in the way.

"We can't make sense of it. There's no logic involved like in the natural world. Over in the Grace Greenhouses, we plant radish seed. Would we ever be shocked if beans resulted! Or how about a crop of pansies? It can't happen that way. Somehow we expect the same thing in people. Job was not reaping what he sowed in chapters one through forty-one. The harvest didn't arrive until chapter forty-two, when God exonerates Job and then blesses him with double he had before."

Zane shifted in his seat. He had a lot of blessings. A home without a mortgage. A job that paid the bills. Friends like Tony.

"Our story and the story of our fallen world doesn't end until it's over, either. Scripture doesn't negate the principle. Let's go back to Paul's letter to the Galatian church. 'Whoever sows to please their flesh, from the flesh will reap destruction,' he told them. 'Whoever sows to please the Spirit, from the Spirit will reap eternal life.'"

Zane had listened to that passage on his phone just the other day.

"If we sow faith and trust in Jesus, we will harvest eternal life. So why is there evil in this world? Why does

God allow it to remain? We question, don't we? God speaks clearly at the end of the book of Job. 'Who is this that obscures my plans with words without knowledge?' He goes on for two chapters asking Job if he was there when the Earth's foundations were laid, when the morning stars sang together and the angels shouted for joy. If Job could bind the constellations or control the weather or tame the leviathan. And Job had to answer in the negative. He wasn't God. Only God was God."

The words hit Zane like a sledgehammer. He'd done a lot of internal whining about his hard life but, in the context of the creation of the universe, it was nothing.

"Let that sink in for a minute. We can rail against God for allowing evil. If things had turned out differently for Officer Sinclair — if she'd been ushered into God's presence on Friday — would God have been any less good? No, my friends. We cannot begin to understand. Even Job said at the end, 'Surely I spoke of things I did not understand, things too wonderful for me to know. My ears had heard of you, but now my eyes have seen you.'"

Pastor Ivan paused and looked out at the quiet congregation.

"Why does God allow evil? If there's any message from the story of Job, it's that we cannot understand the mind of God. We have to trust. Our choice lies between believing we know better than God and thus rejecting Him, or believing He sees the big picture. You may have trials in your life. In fact, I'm sure you have asked God, 'why me? Why did You allow this problem or that one into my life?' And His answer is simply, 'do you trust Me, my child? Continue to sow faith and trust, and you will reap the harvest of eternal life.' Let us pray."

Zane bowed his head.

There are no guarantees. Life's short.

That was all Kenia could think of as Pastor Ivan's sermon wrapped up. How would Jonah have reacted if Gloria had died? It wasn't like Kenia wanted him back, but she still cared about him as a human being. He'd been so cheerful on Friday, more relaxed than she'd ever seen him. That hadn't just been the exhaustion speaking.

She shot a glance across the sanctuary to where Zane sat beside Tony, his face grave. Did he know Gloria, or was he thinking of something else? His gaze met hers and held for several seconds. Caught in the intensity, breath left her.

Between them, Nancy Poncetta and her daughter-in-law rose, gathering their purses and Bibles, breaking the contact.

Alaina touched Kenia's arm. "Wow. That was powerful."

It took a second for Kenia to realize her friend spoke

of the sermon, not the smoldering exchange. "Yes."

"I'm sure glad Gloria is going to be okay. How is it affecting you?"

"Me?" Kenia stared at her friend. "I'm glad, too. You think I'd want something bad to happen to her in hopes of Jonah coming back to me? That's crazy talk."

"No, that's not what I meant at all."

"What then?"

"I wondered if you wanted to talk about it."

Kenia shook her head. "There's nothing to talk about. Any feelings I had for Jonah are long gone. They weren't that strong to begin with, not compared to—" She pressed her lips tight.

Alaina's eyebrows rose. "Compared to what, Kenia?"

Nope. Not going there. Definitely not with Cameron slipping his arm around his wife and leaning forward to see Kenia's face and hear her response. She shook her head.

"The Sunrise?" asked Cameron.

"Sure." Anything to change the subject. "It's either that or going to my parents' house, and I'm not up for that." If Alaina would probe, Mom would be a thousand times worse. Why couldn't they all see the seeds of her love for Jonah — and she used the word lightly — had fallen on dry ground and withered away? There was no harvest in that direction. She didn't even want one.

Cameron looked up past Kenia's shoulder. "Hey, I

was going to come look for you guys. Lunch at the Sunrise?"

She froze, closed her eyes, and took a deep breath filled with the essence of Zane. She hadn't acted yet on her bravado of the other day. Maybe she wouldn't need to. Life held no guarantees. Maybe he'd caught the same message she had.

Kenia glanced up. He was so near, his hand resting on the back of the pew close enough to her shoulder she could almost feel the heat, his eyes burning into hers. She offered him a tentative smile, hoping he'd catch the message. His eyebrows lifted, and she nodded slightly.

"I'd like that," he said, more to her than to Cameron.

Alaina's elbow grazed Kenia's ribs, but she resisted the impulse to glower at her friend. She stood, her gaze still trapped in Zane's as she stepped into the aisle.

"See you there, then." Alaina's chuckle was joined by Cameron's.

Zane touched the small of Kenia's back and stayed close behind her as they wended their way through the crowded foyer and out into the April sunshine. Then he stuffed his hands in his pockets and stood still on the sidewalk. "I need to talk to you."

She smiled up at him. "Go ahead."

"This is hard."

What was so difficult about asking a girl out? He had to know her answer would be different this time. That the connection went both ways. She tucked her hand around his arm and tugged him to walking. "It's not far to the Sunrise. Want to walk?"

"Uh, sure. We can come back later for our vehicles." He fell into step beside her.

She could talk about the weather. About the sermon. About the weekly excursions to the greenhouse... but then when would he open up? She chomped down on her bottom lip to keep her mouth shut.

They'd turned the corner at the end of the block before he spoke. "There's something you need to know about me."

Married ten years ago and never divorced? In league with Gloria's shooter? Kenia waited.

"I can't read."

He *what*? Kenia's feet stopped as she turned to stare at him. He still looked normal. One head, not two. One very cute head with dark eyes begging for understanding. "How...? I don't understand."

"Well, not *can't* exactly. I can figure stuff out, but it's really hard. My parents, my teachers, everyone said I was just lazy. I'm not lazy, Kenia."

She shook her head. "No. I know you're not. But—"

"So they labeled me dyslexic. They tried vision therapy. They tried multisensory instruction. They wanted to put me on drugs for ADHD, but I didn't quite fit the pattern."

Kenia's heart went out to the child Zane had been. "I'm sorry. It must have been rough." Reading had always come so easily to her. She'd started when she was five and had rarely been without a book on the go ever since. Life without stories seemed dull and gray, like a world full of pencil sketches but no colors.

"I'm not stupid."

She turned to him and reached for both his hands. "I know."

"Arthur Smythe at the library thinks he can help me."

"Oh, cool! What's his specialty?"

"He's a volunteer who teaches adult literacy. Just an older guy who's been through what I have and found a way to make words stay still long enough to be deciphered."

Interesting wording. She angled her head and stayed focused on Zane's eyes. "How's that?"

"Colored overlays. It sounds silly, I know."

"I wasn't going to say that. It's intriguing. How does it work?"

"They tried it when I was a kid. They had a few plastic sheets to put on top of the paper, different colors, but it didn't help. Arthur says testing for... whatever the syndrome is... has come a long way since then, and there are specialists trained in diagnosing it. They test with hundreds of shades, not just the three or four my therapist had."

"So you're going to give it another try with a specialist?"

He nodded and clenched her hands. "Do you think

I'm crazy to do it? I'll have to take a day off work and drive to Pocatello."

"Truth? I'd think you were crazy not to."

"What if it doesn't help?"

"But what if it does?"

"I'm serious. Even this tiny bit of hope is scaring me. Maybe it's better just to accept how God made me."

"Zane." She stepped closer, right into his space. He was only a breath away. "Whether this specialist can help or not doesn't change your worth."

"But I can't read."

Yeah, reading was important. She, of all people, got that. But the hang-dog expression on his face punched her deep. "You know I love books. I love information. I love stories. I love being transported to faraway places to experience things I can't in real life. But, Zane, there's more to life. Embrace it."

His hands slid up her arms, and she shivered slightly. "Are you cold?" His voice was quiet, a little husky.

It might only be mid-April, but that had nothing to do with her need for the warmth only he could provide. She shifted that tiny bit closer and wrapped her arms around his waist as his hands pulled her in. "Not anymore," she murmured against his chest.

Chapter 13

*T*HOUGHT YOU'D NEVER get here." Tony's hand clapped Zane's shoulder.

Zane glanced over at the table by the window and caught Alaina's knowing grin, while her husband seemed busy with the twins. He loosened his grip on Kenia's hand, but she tightened hers. Okay, if that's how she wanted it, he wouldn't complain.

Wait, everyone must have driven by on their way to the café while he and Kenia had been gazing into each other's eyes. At least they hadn't been kissing... although he'd like to give that a try, and soon.

He held out a chair for her then seated himself next to her, amazed at the flash of a brilliant smile she tossed him. He basked in the warm glow of it. He'd been so sure she'd laugh at him or walk away, or... or *something*. He hadn't expected compassion. Not even after Tony. After Arthur Smythe.

Kenia smoothed the napkin on her lap and looked around the table, chin up. "Yes, for those who are so obviously wondering what's going on, Zane invited me to a concert in Twin Falls Friday night, and I said yes."

"It's about time," murmured Alaina.

Wait, had she really said that? Zane's ears burned.

"Agreed." Tony chuckled. "I hope you're coming to Italiana for dinner first."

"Can I get you something to drink?" The waitress stood at the end of the table, a bright smile on her face.

"I'll have a coffee," announced Evan. "With lots of sugar."

Cameron lightly cuffed his son's head. "I think not."

The boy turned imploring eyes at his dad. "Is it because I forgot to say please?"

"No, it's because you're seven years old, and it will stunt your growth." Cameron turned back to the waitress. "Orange juice for the boys, please. I'll have a coffee, with cream and no sugar." He glanced at Alaina. "What about you, love?"

Evan slumped into his chair, scowling, and Zane couldn't help chuckling at the smug expression on Oliver's face as his stepmom gave her order. Those two were something else. They certainly kept things hopping on Tuesday afternoons at the greenhouse between pestering the girls and helping Clarence so much he got annoyed with their interference.

"Peppermint mocha, no whip," Kenia said to the waitress.

She couldn't possibly think she needed to lose weight? She was so slender he'd almost been able to wrap his hands around her waist. He'd finally had the chance to try. He shifted slightly in his chair. This was too good to be true. He'd dumped his biggest woe on her and she'd barely blinked. Had she not understood? Zane replayed the conversation. No, he'd made it clear.

Suddenly he felt as light as air. Maybe he was the one who needed sugar and cream in his coffee for once. Maybe he needed weight to anchor himself against the billowing feelings inside his chest. He couldn't help the grin that crept to his face. Nah, he was solid. No danger of floating away, regardless of the unfamiliar emotions. He'd give her time to come to her senses before giving into belief.

Everyone added their meal selections before the waitress left the table.

Kenia leaned forward and surveyed the table. "I have a question for you guys."

Uh oh.

"It looks like I'm buying Page Turners from my aunt, and..."

Zane's brain blanked. He tried to envision himself dating a bookstore owner, but no picture came to mind. Bad enough she worked there, but to own it? How could he even think of a future with this woman? Not that marriage was on the table. Not yet, at any rate, but why set himself up for failure?

No. That was the old Zane speaking. The one who was down on himself and hiding behind a façade of perfection. He knew her life revolved around books. Had known it all along.

"...tearing out the wall and expanding into the other half. Maybe punching a couple of windows through on the Washington Street side. What do you think?"

He'd missed it all. Missed the crux of her question.

"That would give you room for a lot more inventory, but how much more can you sell?" Tony asked. "Arcadia Valley is a fairly small town for a big bookstore."

"I was thinking of a coffee shop, meeting area, and maybe a section for local crafts." Kenia's hand rested on Zane's knee. "Most bookstores have a bit wider selection than what we've had space for."

She remembered that conversation from way back in February? He wrapped his fingers around hers.

"The only coffee shop in the downtown core is The Beanery," Alaina observed. "Demi's Delights is more of a tea room, and then there's the Jukebox and here. Could work."

"Games," announced Cameron. "That's what's missing in Arcadia Valley — a store with a good selection of board games for all ages. We had to order online for the twins' Christmas gifts."

"I thought Santa gave us Quirkle," put in Evan.

Oliver elbowed him. "That was Mom, silly."

"No, Mom bought us the Wilderking books, remember? Quirkle was from Santa."

Cameron sighed. "The books *and* the games were from Mom and me. We've talked about Santa."

Everyone chuckled.

"So, games," said Kenia. "Good idea. I could even have a few out for people to play right there. Chess, checkers. Maybe others."

"You could host murder mystery dinners," put in Alaina. "Those are for eight players and a lot of fun."

"I don't want to cater meals, though. I can't cook, remember?"

Alaina laughed. "Evenings by special appointment, then. A dessert tray with the last act would be perfect."

"Hmm. A coffee shop needs a few goodies. Cookies or tarts or something. Maybe this is a bad idea."

"You can't do everything anyway," said Alaina. "You keep running the bookstore part and hire someone as a barista. Maybe you can get a selection of sweets every morning from A Slice of Heaven or Demi's."

What was the expression that swept across Kenia's face? Zane couldn't read it before it slipped away. There was so much about her he didn't know.

The waitress set plates around the table. Cameron asked Tony to pray over their meal then the chatter quieted as everyone dug into their meals. Even the twins were too busy to make noise.

Zane missed the warmth of Kenia's hand in his, but it would happen again. She'd agreed to go out with him to that concert. Maybe he'd take her to Italiana for dinner first, like Tony suggested. With God's help, he was going to do everything right so she'd fall in love with him. Just like the sermon this morning. If he sowed all the stuff women liked — flowers, chocolate, romantic dates — he'd reap love and commitment. Someone who'd stand beside him for the long haul.

It wouldn't happen overnight. Nothing worth its salt grew that quickly. But the seeds had been sown and, just like the tiny seedlings in the greenhouse, were beginning to sprout.

Kenia strolled through Arcadia Creek Park hand-in-hand with Zane. She and Jonah had come a time or two, but this was different. Not only were early crocuses poking through the lawn in a happy array of yellow and purple, so too were the jonquil shoots ready to bloom. Back in January, snow had covered the entire park. She couldn't kick herself anymore that she'd wasted time on Jonah. She'd learned a few things during those six weeks, and not only that a man who could cook was a wondrous thing.

Could Zane? It didn't even matter. That's what takeout was for. Or maybe the expanded bookstore would do so well she could be like her mother and hire a cook... although visions of her and Zane puttering around the little kitchen in the upstairs apartment had a certain amount of appeal right there.

She breathed in the fresh spring air and exhaled a happy breath.

Zane's arm slipped around her waist, making her glad she wore a light jacket rather than a heavy parka. She wrapped her arm around him and matched her step to his.

"I've dreamed of this," she murmured.

He stopped on the path and turned toward her. "You have?"

"You needn't sound so surprised. I might have said no the first time, but that was months ago, and I didn't even know you then."

"I rushed you, and then I ran, afraid."

"Afraid of what?"

"Afraid of a woman who manages a bookstore." His fingers traced her cheek. "Afraid I could never measure up."

She had to know. "Did you really give away the stack of books you'd bid on?"

His grin turned lopsided and the dimple appeared. "I really did. I told you I panicked."

"Why did you bid on a romance package?"

"I didn't look that closely. All I knew was you looked sad that night, and I felt an instant connection with you. Bidding on your donations seemed the only way to meet you." He shook his head. "Told you I wasn't thinking straight."

"It was a rough evening. I broke up with my boyfriend the day before." At least it had been her that had done the deed.

His hand dropped to his side, and she felt the instant chill before she grabbed his fingers. "I promise you, we were never meant to be. He's a nice enough guy, but we weren't in love. I'd been kind of hoping we might get there, but that day I knew it would never happen."

"How could anyone not love you?"

Kenia stared at him. Had he really just said that? His intense gaze bored into hers. "I'm not always lovable, Zane. I talk too much and I'm impulsive. And I can't cook."

"I know." A little humor gleamed in those dark eyes. "But I'm still here."

Which did he know? That she talked too much, or that she couldn't cook? Her mind slid back to that day in the greenhouse and what he must have overheard of her conversation with Evelyn. "How about you? Can you cook?"

"I can make good stuff, so long as I don't need a recipe." He gave a rueful grin. "Hard when you can't read well."

"We could give it a try together."

"I'd like that. I have a big kitchen."

"I don't even know where you live."

"My grandparents left me their house when they passed on. It's just a few blocks north of here. Tony and Quinn rent rooms from me."

"And I'm in a little rental near El Corazon. It has no kitchen to speak of. But the building downtown comes with a decent apartment upstairs, so I'll move in there, probably sometime this summer. It needs a bit of work."

"That's a big step, buying not only a business but an entire building."

Kenia looked down. "My parents are pitching in, no strings attached."

"Must be nice."

"Yeah, it is." She took a deep breath and looked at him again. "They've got money and, since I'm allergic to the family business, they're helping me out. My mom still sounds like she thinks I could just decide not to have a sinus attack in the flower shop, but she's wrong."

"So you're allergic to flowers?"

She pointed at the daffodil buds nearby. "Not in the wild. It's all the chemicals needed to make perfect blossoms for retail."

"You make it easy for a guy."

"What do you mean?"

"Flowers could take up a lot of a dating budget." He grimaced. "I mean, not that I'm budgeting, exactly."

Kenia chuckled as his expression fell. "No, you'll have to get more creative. And my last boyfriend owned a bakery, so cookies don't cut it, either. I'm tough to please."

Zane's hands rested on her hips for a second before sliding around her waist. "You'll have to give me some ideas. What do you like?"

He was so close her senses filled with his essence. Rational thought was a distant dream.

"I like walks in the moonlight," she whispered. "Dancing in the rain. Cozy evenings by the fire."

"We can do that." His hands tightened, drawing her closer.

Kenia wrapped her arms around his neck. "I like kissing."

Those dark eyes smoldered, gazing deep before she closed hers. His lips swept hers and then branded her forehead, leaving her entire body reeling in a shockwave.

"That's not quite what I meant," she murmured. She tangled her fingers in his hair and drew his lips back into range with a little tug. "Kiss me."

He did. He kissed her slowly and thoroughly, holding her up though her knees buckled. The spring breeze, the crocuses and green shoots and the entire park faded away. Kissing Jonah had never been like this. That should have been her first clue.

The warmth of Zane's arms encompassed her and

the breath of his being filled her.

Suddenly she couldn't wait to see what happened next.

Chapter 14

IN PERSON OR BY PHONE? There were pros and cons both ways. One thing Kenia knew — it couldn't be put off. The Arcadia Valley grapevine moved too quickly for that, and her mother would never forgive her if that's how she found out.

Kenia lifted her phone. No, that was the chicken's way out. It was late Sunday afternoon, so surely her parents were home. Maybe Dad would even be a buffer. Yeah, right. But if she told them both at the same time, she wouldn't be at the mercy of Mom's spin when she told Dad. That settled it.

She jammed her phone back in her purse and headed back out to her Ford Fiesta. A few clouds had rolled in since the glorious sun-soaked hours in the park. She rounded the bend in the drive through The Cottages and waved at Mariana Peters, who was outside poking at her flowerbeds.

In just a few minutes she'd pulled into the circle drive in front of her parents' imposing Georgian with its perfect grounds, already green in mid spring. Her brother's cherry red Eos stood beside the curving brick walkway, and Kenia exhaled a breath she hadn't realized she'd been holding. She could count on Grady and Joanna to support her. Joanna, at least.

Kenia breezed through the front door into the walnut-paneled foyer and came face-to-face with a humungous floral arrangement on the mahogany hall table. The mass of daffodils and tulips must be three feet tall. "Hello?" she called.

Her mother, dressed in a silk skirt and jacket and every hair in place, appeared in the doorway to the den. "Kenia, darling. We weren't expecting you."

Kenia kicked off her heels and crossed the marble floor to give her mother a hug. "I hope it's okay I dropped by."

"Of course. Your brother just arrived. He says he has something to tell us."

"Is it private? Maybe I should come back." Even though she was pretty sure what Grady's revelation might be, Mom didn't know that.

"Kenia?" called Grady. "Come on in."

"If you're sure."

"Absolutely."

Mom pursed her lips slightly, stepped aside to usher Kenia into the den, and sat on the edge of a tufted Victorian chair. "Well, both our children home at the same time. Neither needed an invitation. Once Lucia has brought tea and squares, you may go ahead, Grady, as you were here first."

To say nothing of him being the son and the heir. Whatever. Their mother valued the trappings of wealth.

Joanna rose from her seat beside Grady on the leather loveseat and gave Kenia a brief hug. "Nice to see you. How was church this morning? I didn't feel well, so we stayed home."

"Good." Kenia wracked her brain to remember church. It had been before lunch and the afternoon in the park. "Pastor Ivan preached from the book of Job. Good sermon. You should find it online later."

"I'm glad you were listening, darling." Mom nodded at Dad as they shared a smile.

Lucia entered with a well-loaded tray bearing five teacups. The kitchen had already gotten wind of Kenia's arrival. Impressive.

Mom took a sip of her tea, but as soon as Lucia left the room, her gaze flitted from Kenia to Grady. "Go ahead, son."

Grady's fingers tightened around his wife's. "We wanted to let you know you'll be grandparents. Our baby is due in mid-September."

"That's wonderful." Mom's gaze darted to Dad then

back to Grady. "We're very happy for you. I suppose now that your father and I are nearly ready to retire, we're old enough to have a grandchild."

Good grief. Kenia managed not to snort. Her brother was old enough to have a ten-year-old. "Congrats to you!" She poured enthusiasm into her words. "I can hardly wait to spoil your little one rotten. I'll be the fun auntie." The baby's other aunt would be Joanna's brother Cameron's wife. For some reason, Kenia had never thought of Alaina and her sharing nieces and nephews. "Any books you want for the nursery, you just let me know."

"Yes, congratulations." Dad rounded the desk and shook Grady's hand before stretching both of his toward Joanna. "This is wonderful news."

Joanna rose and gave Dad a tentative hug before sinking down beside Grady again and shooting Kenia a small smile.

Did other families suffer from this kind of stiffness? Hmm, that was one thing she didn't know about Zane. He'd mentioned his grandparents, but not his parents or any siblings. Well, she couldn't expect to discover everything about him in one amazing afternoon.

"Boy or girl?" Dad asked, resuming his seat.

The couple exchanged a glance. "We don't know," Grady said. "And we're not sure we want to find out in advance. Where's the fun in that?"

Mom set her teacup down and leaned forward.

"Knowing would make decorating the nursery so much easier, to say nothing of shopping for baby clothes. I really think you should—"

"Linda." Dad shook his head.

Good for him, stopping the lecture. Yes, having him here would make all the difference for her, too.

"Kenia, did you say you had something to tell us as well?" Dad's eyes focused on Kenia. "Let's hope the news is quite different."

She stared at him. "Of course, it is. I can't believe you even said that."

"It was a transition." He shook his head. "Go ahead."

Kenia squeezed her eyes tight for a second and wished she had someone here to hold her hand like Grady held Joanna's, but that was ridiculous. These were her parents. They loved her and wanted what was best for her. "I've met someone, and I wanted to tell you about him before the town gossip reached you."

Mom's eyes narrowed. "That does not sound like you've come to your senses about Jonah Baxter."

Way to throw a damper on things. "Mom, what part of *he's in love with someone else* did you miss? No, I'm not getting back together with Jonah. I'm sure you heard his girlfriend got shot on Friday but is expected to recover with no problems. I imagine it won't be long before their wedding bells start ringing."

"I'm sorry to hear that."

"Let's hear about the new young man in her life,

Linda. Go ahead, Kenia."

"His name is Zane Russell, and he works at Retro Village. Granddad really likes him, and—"

"I thought the director's name was Mr. Davis. A middle-aged man."

Kenia stared at her mother. "Yes, but what does that have to do with anything?"

Mom's hands fluttered. "Go ahead. What does this Zane do there, if he's not the director?"

"He's the activities coordinator. He—"

"He's not even a nurse? Just someone who tells Blake Taylor when to bring the therapy dogs by?"

Wait until Mom found out Zane struggled with reading. Well, she'd never hear it from Kenia. "His job is more important than that, and he's good at it."

Dad cleared his throat. "As a Retro Village board member, I'm aware of Mr. Russell's employment situation. I'm not at liberty to give any details, of course, but things are not as secure as you may have been led to believe. I also know his salary. Kenia, I think you'd do well to let this go and find someone else."

She shot to her feet. "Someone more worthy of an Akers?" Some days she hated her parents.

They exchanged a look.

"I wouldn't put it that way," Dad said slowly. "But someone who can hold his own and doesn't need you to support him."

"I'm buying commercial property and a thriving

business. Don't you think I can support myself, my husband, and a dozen kids if I choose to? But it isn't that way. Whatever you think of Zane, he works hard. He's not the kind to mooch off someone else." Kenia pivoted at the den door. "I thought you'd be happy for me, or at least cautiously optimistic. I'll see myself out."

For two days, Zane wondered what he'd done wrong Sunday afternoon. The kissing had definitely been mutual. Kenia had even started it, so the unusual quiet from her couldn't be because he'd pushed her and gone too far. Unless it had been a test.

He weighed that thought as he watched the seniors and the kids interact in the greenhouse Tuesday afternoon. Kenia was glued to her grandfather's side, guiding his hands as he transplanted tiny sprouts into larger trays. She'd given him a fleeting smile with her hello, but barely met his eyes.

Something was definitely wrong, and all he could think of was that she'd had time to reassess his life as a nonreader. Maybe she'd decided he wasn't worth the bother, after all. She owned a bookstore. She loved to read. She'd said so herself. He'd heard her and Tony and Alaina banter books at the Sunday lunch table.

Even if Arthur Smythe was telling the truth — and Tony's research had borne it up — there was no guarantee this therapy would make any difference at all. Hadn't he tried colored overlays as a child? The black letters had wavered just as much under blue, green, or pink as they had on white.

"This is a great program." Cheri's voice came from beside his shoulder. "I'm so glad you thought of it. The kids really look forward to Tuesdays."

Was this where he told her it hadn't even been his idea? And not only that, but two months had gone by and he still needed to find and launch more programs or lose his job. It wasn't like Arcadia Valley had all the amenities of a larger city... but there was no need to dump his burdens on the daycare worker. "Thanks. It's the highlight of the residents' week, too."

"Mixing kids, seniors, and gardens. Brilliant. I know my grandparents brighten up when they can take my daughter in their garden to pick vegetables or berries."

Zane didn't really know anything about Cheri. This was the first time she'd talked to him beyond what the group was doing on any given day. He poked his chin toward the bustling greenhouse. "Your daughter is in here?"

She shook her head. "She just turned five, so she's in the other group. It's nice she can be at the same facility where I work, though. We can spend a few minutes together here and there throughout the day."

Sounded like a single mom. There seemed to be a lot of them around these days. Women abandoned by their men. Or, yeah, sometimes the other way around, like in Cameron's case. What a world of mixed-up kids. "Your grandparents can't help care for her?"

"They're ranching in Montana, so, no."

"Evannnn!" Ophelia drew out the boy's name while she looked around, trying to catch the eye of an adult. Thankfully, not Zane's responsibility.

Cheri sighed. "Those two. Always at each other's throats." She strode toward the little girl. "What seems to be the problem?"

Kenia glanced over at the children but didn't leave Clarence's side. Her gaze caught on Zane's when she turned back and held for a long moment. Her beautiful mouth tilted to one side in a rueful grin. Maybe she was just as thankful not to be responsible for the Kraus boy, even though his twin hovered so close to Clarence's other elbow that the old man had clipped the boy's head a time or two.

Zane made his way down the gravel path, never taking his eyes off her. He stopped close beside her, his arm pressed against hers as he leaned onto the potting table and angled a look around her at the old man. "How's it going, Clarence?"

His world tilted upright just from the heat of her arm against his. *You're a goner, Russell.* Might be true, but he couldn't make himself mind.

The old man's cloudy eyes met his, shifted to Kenia's, then back. "Who're you?"

"Zane. I drove the bus that brought you here to the greenhouse." He knew better than to try to prompt any of the residents to remember. Sometimes, the moment they were in was the only moment that existed.

"Oh." Clarence looked at Kenia. "What a nice young man. Is he yours?"

From the other side, Oliver snickered. "They're kissy faces."

Uh oh. What had the boy seen, and when?

Kenia's cheeks flushed, but she didn't look up at Zane.

"Eh? What's that?" blustered Clarence.

"We went to the park to play catch with Dad and saw them smooching." The boy made smacking sounds. "Dad said it wasn't polite to stare."

So then the boys' stepmom, Kenia's friend, knew. But everyone had already heard at Sunday lunch that they were going out this week, so a few kisses in the park wouldn't be a huge shock. More than a few kisses that had rocked Zane's entire universe.

"Smooching?" Clarence's voice rang out across the greenhouse.

A few children tittered. Several the residents peered over as though trying to catch a glimpse of the action.

Here went nothing. "Smooching is a lot of fun," Zane told the boy. "But I don't recommend it until you're a grownup."

"Evan smooched Ophelia," Oliver said with a tilt to

his head. "But she smacked him."

Zane couldn't help himself. He slipped his arm around Kenia's waist, keeping his gaze on Oliver. Hard to do as he inhaled the essence of Kenia. "That can happen if a boy tries to steal kisses. It's really better if you know for sure the girl wants to kiss you back." He shook his head, brushing against Kenia's short hair. "It's not fun when a girl hits you."

Oliver's eyes widened. "Did a girl hit you? Did it hurt? Evan had a bloody nose."

Wow, Ophelia packed a wicked punch for an angelic-looking seven-year-old.

Clarence swayed. "I don't like blood."

This whole thing was getting out of hand. Zane glanced at the greenhouse clock. It was only two minutes before Cheri called story time. He had no problem jumping the gun. It beat swapping smooching and smacking stories with a little kid like Oliver, because once he'd been labeled stupid, the girls at school hadn't wanted anything to do with him.

Chapter 15

*K*ENIA LEANED AGAINST THE wall at the back of the children's center listening to Cheri read a story about a group of vegetables vying to be the favorites, begging to be picked first. Granddad was settled in a chair off to the side near Ida Snyder's wheelchair, frowning at Cheri.

Where had Zane disappeared to? Her body still tingled in all the places he'd touched in the greenhouse, just the pressure of his presence as he chatted with Granddad and Oliver. She'd been avoiding him, kind of, still wrangling her anger at her parents' attitude and uncertain how to handle it even after going down to the Y for a workout on the punching bag. They'd been so sure Joanna was a gold digger at first. Now they thought the same of Zane. That he was beneath an Akers.

And they didn't even know he couldn't read. Mom would lock Kenia up in a high tower and throw away the key if she found out, and Kenia definitely didn't have Rapunzel's long flowing hair to enable Zane to free her.

Maybe she'd read too many fairy tales.

The sound of the closing patio door caught her attention. Zane. He walked toward her, and she caught her breath. How could one guy embody everything masculine and, well, hot? Those smoldering eyes, the dark, unruly hair, the white T-shirt stretched across a muscled chest.

He leaned beside her a mere inch or two away, arms crossed over his chest, so near she could feel the tantalizing heat from his arm. She lost herself in his eyes then blinked as a slow smile crept across his unshaven cheeks until his dimple was revealed. "Do you want to talk about it?"

Kenia could pretend she didn't know what he was talking about, but there was no point in playing games. Yet, what good did it do to dump her woes with her parents on him? She shook her head. "Not really."

Zane shifted slightly away and looked toward Cheri. "Okay."

He read it as rejection. Of course he did. She bumped his arm. "It's not that."

"How would I know what it is or isn't?"

A fair point. Kenia shook her head. "It's just my parents being... parents." She'd like to add it had nothing to do with him, and that was partially true... but he wouldn't see it that way.

"I'm not good enough for their little girl?"

Why did he have to be so astute? She grimaced. "I'm not sure anyone would be. There might be a reason my brother didn't marry until he was thirty-three."

Zane regarded her thoughtfully. "They're probably right."

Her eyebrows shot up. "They're probably *not*."

"They want what's best for you."

"Whose side are you on?"

He sighed. "I'm just being realistic. If I had a daughter, I'd want to protect her from guys like me, too."

If he had a daughter... Kenia's mind spun to that vision she'd glimpsed of Zane holding a baby in the upstairs apartment. If he had a daughter, would he cheer her on as she bopped little boys like Evan Kraus on the nose? More to the point, if he had a daughter, would Kenia be the mother?

She studied his profile as Cheri's lilting voice read the climax where the vegetables battled it out until all were minced, sliced, or chopped. "Should I be worried? Do I need someone to protect me from you?"

Zane arched a brow in her direction. "I don't know. Do you?"

"Another story!" called Ophelia.

"I'm sorry, children." Cheri closed the book and set it down. "That's all for right now. Say goodbye to your friends, because it's time for them to return to Retro

Village. We'll meet in the play yard in just a few minutes."

The kids bounced to their feet as the seniors rose more slowly.

Time was up.

Zane leaned closer as the hubbub increased until his lips grazed her ear. "Busy tonight? I find I can't wait until Friday to see you again."

Was she going to let her parents' opinion sway her or not? She'd choose *not*. Kenia turned slightly, but he hadn't allowed her much room. "Do you know where the cottages are near El Corazon? I live in number twelve. Come on over this evening, and we'll go for a walk."

"El Corazon? I have a better idea. Why don't I swing by around six and we can go for dinner?"

Should she let him spend money on dinner when she knew his job might not last much longer? Did *he* know it was in jeopardy? Right. She was going to push that entire conversation with her parents out of her head. "Six sounds good. I love Mexican."

"Veronica!"

Zane should have known. A born-and-bred Arcadian like Kenia would know people all over town, but he hadn't expected his date to rush across the restaurant, grab the hostess, and give her a spin. The two women hugged and whispered for a few seconds before Veronica looked past Kenia's shoulder and smiled at him.

Was that his cue? Probably.

Kenia grabbed his hand when he approached the hostess stand. "Veronica, I'd like you to meet Zane Russell. He works over at Retro Village. Zane, this is Veronica Quintana." Kenia waved a hand to encompass the restaurant. "Of the El Corazon Quintanas. I've known her forever, plus we were neighbors at The Cottages for over a year. And then she moved to Twin Falls, but now she's back, but her cottage is rented out." She turned to her friend and made a moue of disappointment. "I miss having you in the neighborhood."

"I miss it, too." Veronica gave her another quick hug and lifted two menus from the stand. "Nice to meet you, Zane. Table for two? Right over here." She led the way to a spot by the window. "Our special today is a sweet potato and black bean burrito. Our vegetarian options have become very popular."

Vegetarian? Not really Zane's style. He held a chair for Kenia and noted Veronica's quick smile of approval. Then he rounded the table and flipped open his menu. As always, the words wiggled across the page. The special might be better than it sounded. At least it wasn't tofu.

"Can I get you anything to drink? We have watermelon water on tap today."

Kenia gave her friend a wide smile. "That sounds wonderful. Zane?"

His heart stuttered at the sight of her bright eyes turned toward him. "Sure. And a coffee, please."

Her eyes crinkled around the corners. "That'll keep you awake all night."

He grinned back. "It never has yet."

Veronica chuckled. "I'll get your drinks. Your waiter tonight will be David, and he'll be right with you. He can answer any questions you might have about the menu."

Was it bad to feel relief that Kenia's friend wouldn't be hovering over their table chatting Kenia up all evening? Because this was their first date. *First date.* He allowed his mind to savor the words as Kenia bent over her menu.

She glanced up. "What are you thinking of having?"

"Maybe the special. You?"

Her gaze slid to the menu in front of him then back to his eyes. "It's hard to read?"

His gut sank. "Yeah."

"Well, they've got the usual tacos and enchiladas. Quesadillas." She turned the page. "Oh, the Sopa Azteca looks good."

"Aztec Soup?"

Kenia laughed. "A pasilla chile and tomato broth

ladled over crunchy tortilla chips, and topped with avocado, cheese, and cream. Perfection in a bowl."

"Any meat?"

"No, that one's labeled vegetarian as well. You're looking for beef, chicken, or fish?"

"Beef."

"Spoken like a true man." She shot him a quick grin. "How about beef tacos? Shredded brisket served with lime and avocado."

"Sounds perfect." He reached across the table and captured her hand. "Thanks."

Kenia's brows furrowed. "You're welcome? But for what?"

"For telling me what's on the menu. For not making fun of me."

Her hand turned over, and her fingers grasped his. "No problem. Really." Her eyes searched his. "What do you usually order?"

"The special."

She grinned. "Even if it's vegetarian?"

Zane shrugged but couldn't help returning the grin. "I've tried a lot of interesting specials over the years."

"I bet."

He poked his chin toward the menu. "So, what are you having?"

"The special." She winked at him and closed the menu.

A spurt of laughter bubbled out. "Really?"

"Why not? It sounded good. I'm not afraid of a vegetarian meal."

"Who said anything about fear?"

She laughed, and his heart warmed. "The panic on your face when you realized there was no meat in the Sopa Azteca?"

Zane captured her other hand as well. "That wasn't panic."

"How would you describe it then?"

Her skin felt so smooth and warm under his as he caressed the base of her thumb. Her blue eyes shone back at him, and he lost himself in the depths. Was this real? A woman like her, knowing about his handicap, and still willing to be with him? Her lips parted in a smile. All he wanted to do was lean over the table and kiss her or, better yet—

"Here you go." Two glasses of pink liquid landed beside their joined hands, ice cubes clattering. The young waiter glanced from one to the other nervously as he pulled a pad from his pocket. "Uh, are you ready to order?"

Zane withdrew his hands, immediately chilled. "Yes, she'd like the special, and I'd like the shredded beef tacos, please. Any appetizers?" He didn't miss the sharp glance Kenia sent his way but stayed focused on the waiter.

"I'll bring a basket of chips with salsa and guacamole right out. Along with your coffee, sir."

He gave up. "Sounds good."

The waiter stepped away. Kenia stared out the window, her hands wrapped around the tall glass.

The moment was gone. But the woman wasn't.

The late April evening was cool when they exited El Corazon an hour later. Kenia drew her jacket tighter around her shoulders.

"Cold?" Zane murmured. He wrapped his arm around her waist. "Is that better?"

She closed her eyes for a second and leaned against his shoulder. "So much." Then she slipped her arm around him and matched her step to his.

They ambled for a block or two in silence, Kenia reveling in his nearness. She might have teased him about being such a man in his search for a beef option on the menu, but that was a minor show of his masculinity. Everything about him from his rugged good looks to his woodsy scent to the firmness of his muscles kept her senses on full alert.

He was everything her heart had been looking for. She could fall for this man. She could fall hard, and that scared her. Ten years of dating. Ten years of casual relationships and some, like Jonah, where she'd hoped for more. Could she trust herself? Her parents didn't think so, but they'd been wrong about Joanna. She was amazing for Grady. Still, Joanna operated her own consulting business. It was small, but at least she hadn't been in a dead end job like Zane's.

But when he had the right color of overlays, he'd be able to read easily, and then he could do any job he set his mind on. He was plenty bright enough. But what if... what if this color therapy didn't work for him? What if he was stuck doing menial work all his life? Would that matter to her?

No... she didn't think so, but how could she know? Besides, the bookstore could support a family. She was sure of it.

Kenia glanced up at Zane. "Have you made your appointment in Pocatello yet?"

He grimaced. "Not yet."

"What are you waiting for?" She nudged him. "Christmas?"

"I'll call soon."

She'd teased him about fear, but this was his real dread. That he'd get his hopes up only to have them dashed forever. "Sometimes it's better to get things over with. Then you know where you stand."

"Sometimes it's better not to know."

Did he really believe that? What would it be like, living life on the edge just in case the middle of the party wasn't all it was cracked up to be? The concept was foreign. She'd always been an embrace-the-fun kind of girl. It had given her a bit of a reputation for a while and backfired at times — Jonah came to mind again — but there had been plenty of rewards. The friends she'd made at University of Utah, managing Page Turners, teaching Sunday school at Grace Fellowship.

She lived a full life, but she yearned for love. Love like her parents had, demanding as they might be. Like Joanna and Grady. Like Evelyn and Ben. Even like Alaina and Cameron, rowdy twins and all.

Kenia slid her hand up and down on Zane's lightweight jacket and felt his grip tighten. "You set up the appointment, and I'll take the day off and go with you. We can make a day of it."

"You'd do that for me?"

"Sure. If you take me to the mall." He stilled, and she laughed. "Kidding. Unless you want to, of course."

Zane turned to her on the sidewalk. "A day with you sounds amazing. I can even manage half an hour at the mall if it will make you happy."

Laughter burst out of her. "Half an hour? Are you some kind of crazy?"

He gathered her in both his arms and looked deeply into her eyes. "Maybe I am. Crazy for you."

Kenia raised herself on tiptoes and swept her lips over his. "That's a kind of crazy that might go both ways."

"Might?" His eyes darkened in the twilight. "Do you mind if I erase all doubt?" He dropped kisses from her temple down her cheek and across her jaw.

Her knees weakened. "You missed," she whispered. "If you want to make sure, you need better aim."

His lips came down on hers, firm. Persuasive.

Consider the doubt erased.

Chapter 16

"THIS IS NICE." Kenia cast an appreciative glance around the Italian restaurant.

"I haven't eaten here before, but Tony often cooks at the house, so I'm sure it will be amazing." Zane rested his hand on the small of her back as they followed the hostess to a table for two set in a brick-lined alcove. He wasn't about to tell her his housemate had insisted dinner tonight was on him.

"Your waiter will be with you in a minute." The hostess smiled and backed away.

"No menu?" Kenia wondered.

Zane grinned. "We're having the special."

She wrinkled her nose at him. "But I like to see the choices."

"Tony says we'll love it."

"Tony knows we're here?" Kenia glanced around.

Zane nodded. Was she having second thoughts about

dating him instead of his friend? Tony, the perfect guy who loved reading and could make magic in the kitchen?

Her shoulders relaxed as her hands reached for Zane's. Whew. He'd take it.

"Okay, then. I'll trust you."

His heart forgot to beat. *How did I get so lucky, Lord?* But it wasn't luck. It was God's timing. His blessing, maybe. "I won't let you down." His gaze held hers.

"See that you don't." Her warning, accompanied as it was by a wink, made him grin.

"I'll blame Tony if something goes wrong. Although I didn't ask if you had allergies."

"Besides to the chemicals in the flower shop?"

He tilted his head. "Besides that." Didn't a person who had one sensitivity often have more? But there was no need to borrow trouble.

"No allergies. I'll eat anything, so long as I don't have to cook it. Beef, chicken, vegetarian — I'm not picky."

Zane chuckled. "Touché."

"So, about Pocatello..."

Only the sure knowledge she'd ask again had pushed him to make the phone call. "May fifteenth at two o'clock."

Her face lit up. "You called!"

He squeezed her hands. "Oh ye of little faith."

Warranted, but still.

"I'll make sure Aunt Irene can cover for me that day."

"How are things going with buying her out?"

"Good. We've set the date for July thirty-first. That gives me some time to draw up plans for expanding into the other half. I was thinking of giving Drew Harrison a call for a quote on the renovation. Do you know him?"

"I do." Zane nodded. "He gave me the advice I needed to do some work on my house. Checked in on me a time or two during the process."

The waiter set two glasses of water on the table from the tray held high, then a plate holding a fragrant loaf and a bowl swirling with olive oil and balsamic vinegar. He smiled and nodded.

"Thank you." Kenia beamed at the young man as he backed away. "That smells amazing."

Right, her previous boyfriend had been a baker. Zane shook his head. She'd broken up with him, and she certainly didn't kiss like a woman with divided attention.

He tore the bread in half and offered her a chunk of it. The flavor was distractingly delicious, and so were the zucchini fritters that followed.

"I haven't seen your house yet." Kenia returned to the previous conversation.

"Want to come over on Sunday? I can't promise whether Tony or Quinn will be home or not, but I'll fix lunch for you. Unless that table at the Sunrise Café has your name carved on it every Sunday after church."

She wrinkled her nose at him. "For years I went to my parents' house every week. Then when I dated Jonah..." Her voice drifted away.

"That's when the Sunrise started?" he asked lightly.

Kenia shook her head. "No, Jonah cooks this huge meal for his siblings and their families every Sunday. My parents were all in favor of me dating Jonah, so they didn't complain about the change. They started making other plans for after church, and we've never quite resumed."

Alarm bells rang. "They thought he was the right guy for you?" Because Zane couldn't agree.

She toyed with her napkin. "I guess they did. They really liked that he owns his own business — well, him and his brothers — and has good prospects."

Unlike Zane. His gut tightened. They'd expressed reservations about their little girl seeing him. He felt the whirlpool tugging at him. No. Kenia liked him, and her parents would come around. Maybe he'd soon be reading fluently, and they'd never need to know. He wouldn't push when to meet them. It wasn't like he wanted her to meet *his* parents any time soon, after all.

Zane took a deep breath. "So, about Drew Harrison."

She looked over at him. "Yes. Good reputation as a builder, with lots of experience renovating heritage buildings like the store."

"Sounds like a project he'd love. He's really busy, though. You'll need to talk to him soon. Do you have a second choice of contractor?"

"You think he might not have time?"

"It's hard to know. Last time we talked, he mentioned several big projects coming up. It definitely doesn't hurt to talk to him and get an idea."

"I really don't want to put it off. I'd like the renovation complete before things get busy in the fall."

"Then call Drew, but keep in mind you might need a backup plan. Either waiting, or hiring someone else."

Kenia wrinkled her nose.

An Akers probably didn't need a backup plan often. She talked openly about her previous boyfriend. Did that make Zane the backup plan? The doubts wouldn't leave him alone. What had happened to that suave confident guy who'd bid on the silent auction items on Valentine's Day? He'd ducked and hidden as soon as the initial act of bravado had been rebuffed.

"Dinner for two." The waiter set two empty plates down then a heaped platter of pasta, zoodles, shrimp, meatballs, and more. "Chef Tony invites you to enjoy your meal."

Zane's stomach growled, and Kenia giggled. He reached for her hand. "Let me say the blessing."

Kenia pulled up behind Zane's truck in a residential area a few blocks north of downtown. The older two-story house was clothed in pristine white clapboard and sat on a foundation of native basalt. Green grass sloped gently toward the street, a testament to both good care and the arrival of spring.

Zane opened her car door and held out his hand for her.

She grinned up at him as she climbed out and swung her purse to her shoulder. "Nice house." Well kept. That said something about his character, right there. Sure, it wasn't anywhere near as large as the Craftsman-style house in the southeast that Grady shared with Joanna. Definitely way smaller than her parents' house, but who needed that much space unless they had ten kids?

He ushered her into the spacious interior, and she reassessed her first impression. Most houses of this size and era seemed more cramped. "Oh! Is that where you took out a wall?"

Zane nodded. "Drew coached me how to shore up the opening while still expanding the space. It made a big difference in here."

She turned to take in the kitchen to her left. "This doesn't look like the original cabinetry."

"So true. The kitchen was tiny, ugly, and dark. I'm not sure how my grandmother stood it. They thought it was important to have a separate dining room. I didn't care about that. Who needs two places to eat, really? A little rearrangement, and I was able to double the size of the kitchen."

A *little* rearrangement? Kenia doubted it had been that simple. And there was still plenty of space around the rustic farmhouse table. "I like it." More to the point, the room was so inviting she could even envision cooking in it. Her. The avowed non-chef.

Zane grinned at her. "Have a look around. There's a powder room just around the corner, and the living room is through there. I'll whip us up something to eat."

She couldn't resist the chance to peek at the main floor with its refinished wood floors and light gray walls. A curving staircase with crisp white balusters headed to the second story. If Zane had made the choices and done the work, why wasn't he working for Drew Harrison, or running his own renovation business? Why work at Retro Village?

Because he couldn't read. But once that changed? He'd be free to take wing. He could do anything he wanted.

She rounded the loop and came face-to-face with the kitchen from the other angle. Zane whistled as he sliced bread, a few containers stacked around him. Her heart softened. Did she honestly care if he worked at Retro? Was she as snobbish as her parents? No, she only knew what he might not, that his job was on the line. She wanted what was best for him. It had nothing to do with her.

Kenia slid into a seat at the wide counter. "Anything I can do to help?"

He glanced over, grinning. "I'm keeping it simple. I picked up a loaf of olive bread from A Slice of Heaven and some deli meat and cheese and a jar of home-style soup from Benita's Gourmet Market."

"Sounds like my kind of meal." She'd often popped into Benita's when she and Jonah were dating, since it was in the same plaza as the bakery. "But, I thought you were actually going to cook. You know, from ingredients."

His jaw tensed slightly as he smeared mayo on a slice of bread. "Sorry. I didn't mean to mislead you."

Now she'd gone and done it. "Hey, it's okay. I was just teasing. Benita's has some delicious soups in that back cooler." Kenia came around the end of the counter, bumped up beside him, and tucked her arm around his waist as she reached for the jar. "Mmm. Russian borscht. Great choice."

He kept spreading mayo as she leaned against his shoulder.

"Zane?"

"Hmm?"

She nudged him with her hip. "I'm sorry." Although his reaction seemed over the top.

"Kenia, I..."

Patience. She waited, then tucked her thumb through his belt loop.

"I feel like I'm always whining to you about how hard things are. Truth is, I can cook — it's reading recipes that's challenging." Frustration laced his words. "It's like... I don't know. It's like if you were making something from a cookbook, but every time you turned away to do what you'd just read, someone shut the cookbook without a bookmark. And the recipes rearranged themselves inside the book like some Harry Potter wizarding trick, and you had to find it all over again. Find your place all over again."

He sighed heavily and reached for the package of smoked turkey. "I know that sounds like I'm nuts. And a whiner. That's why I didn't tell anyone for years, just dodged my way around the issue as best I could. I hate sympathy, but I also hate feeling incompetent." He shot her a sideways look. "Especially around an amazing, talented woman."

Kenia took the deli meat from him and set it back on the counter before resting both hands on his hips and drawing him to face her. "You think I'm amazing? That I'm talented? I've got nothing on you, buddy. Have you even *seen* what you've done in this house? Have you even *seen* how much the kids at the greenhouse like you? How the old people respond to you? Granddad lights up when he talks about the program you initiated."

Zane's gaze fixed on hers, almost hungry. Had no one ever told him the stuff he was good at? Yeah, her parents were driven and crazy busy, but they'd loved her and encouraged her, plus she'd had Granddad and Aunt Irene and even her annoying big brother. Together, they'd offered sunshine and rain and a little pruning into her life.

By comparison, Zane had grown up like a weed in a vacant alley.

"Anyone could have done that. It was your idea to bring the kids and the residents together. You wrote up the whole proposal. Because I couldn't."

The day at the Jukebox replayed in her mind. "I didn't suspect at thing."

His eyebrows rose slightly. "I know. *That's* my talent. Keeping people from suspecting."

She could almost hear the words he didn't say. *Keeping people from suspecting how dumb I am.* She shook her head and wrapped her arms around his waist. "Zane, don't be so hard on yourself. You've been fighting a huge battle alone for your entire life." He had, hadn't he? He'd never mentioned his family. Not once. "Tell me about your parents."

"Professors at UC Berkley. Both of them."

Kenia would never have guessed. But wasn't that playing into the stereotype? "I bet you saw them as little as I saw my parents growing up."

"Not a whole lot. Even less when I had trouble in school. They hired me a tutor for a few years, which is the only reason I got as far as I did before dropping out."

Zane looked down at her, his expression hard, his hands clenched at his sides. "Are you sure you want to do this, Kenia? I'm no bargain."

A lot depended on her response right this minute. She could feel the tipping point threatening their precarious balance. "Zane, your problems with reading don't define you. Your education level doesn't define you." In the back of her mind, her parents disagreed with her, but she pushed the thought away. "You're defined by how you live your life. By how you treat your fellow man. But the most important thing is how you respond to God."

His jaw tightened. "I don't always respond well."

Kenia looped her arms around his neck. "None of us do. We're a work in progress. Remember what Pastor Ivan said last week? We harvest what we sow. If we sow negatives, that's what we'll reap. But if we sow the fruits of the Spirit — love, joy, peace, and the rest of them — then we'll harvest the results of that. It's got nothing to do with reading."

His hands came around her as he buried his face against her shoulder.

Kenia held him tight, feeling the strong muscles of his back beneath her hands. She could love this man. The thought startled her in its intensity. She threaded her fingers into his tousled hair, gently kneading his neck and scalp.

After a long moment, Zane lifted his head and looked at her — really looked at her — with moist eyes. "Thank you," he whispered.

And then he kissed her.

Chapter 17

*K*ENIA SQUEALED AND HUGGED her sister-in-law. "You have a baby bump! It's so cute."

Joanna chuckled. "I finally had to realize I wasn't going to be able to wear some of my favorite clothes for a while, so your mom and I went shopping."

"She has good taste." Actually, Mom was opinionated with money to burn, and she'd definitely be showering the heir to the Akers empire lavishly, even if he or she wouldn't be born for a few months yet.

"Yes, she does." Joanna turned to Zane, standing behind Kenia. "Welcome to our house. We're so glad you could join us on Mother's Day."

The moment of truth was about to arrive. Kenia needed to forget the buzz she'd heard this morning at church, that Jonah and Gloria had actually eloped to Vegas a few days ago. She could hardly believe that of think-everything-to-the-death Jonah.

Enough of that. Today was the day she'd introduce Zane to her parents. Their Lexus purred into the paved drive and stopped beside Zane's truck. Dad opened the back door for Mom then rounded the car to help Granddad out of the front passenger seat.

Was it Kenia's imagination, or was her grandfather even frailer than he'd been Tuesday at the greenhouse? He used a walker part of the time, but now he leaned heavily on his son's arm as he shuffled up the walk. How much longer would he be with them? Long enough to hold his great-grandchild in September? Long enough to welcome Kenia's babies?

She tightened her grip on Zane's hand, but he shook it loose as he stepped forward to tuck his hand beneath Granddad's elbow. "Here we go, Clarence. Just two steps up." Between him and Dad, they practically lifted Granddad into the house.

Grady patted the back of a wing chair, and the two men settled Granddad into it then faced each other across it.

Zane stretched out his hand. "I'm Zane Russell, and you must be Kenia's dad."

"Barry Akers." Dad gave Zane's a firm shake, and Kenia dared to snatch a breath. "Thanks for the help with my father."

"No problem. I've gotten to know him quite well through my work at Retro Village. He's a fine man."

Mom's heels clipped up the stone steps, and Kenia

turned to give her a hug. "Hi, Mom."

"Hello, sweetheart." Mom's gaze swept the living area, right over Zane, and came back to Kenia and Joanna. "What can I do to help?"

Joanna gave her mother-in-law a small hug. "Nothing, Linda. It's Mother's Day, and you're our honored guest. Why don't you let Kenia introduce you to her friend, and you can visit while we finish getting the meal on the table?"

Family relations had come a long way since the Mother's Day lunch two years before, when Mom's harsh words had sent Grady's now wife crying to the powder room. Kenia wasn't sure Mom would treat Zane any better today.

"Mom, I'd like you to meet my boyfriend, Zane Russell." First time she'd ever used that word introducing Zane. "Zane, my mother, Linda. I see you've already met my dad." She'd pictured the meeting while holding Zane's hand, not with him across the room.

Mom hesitated, but Zane crossed the space and shook her hand. "Pleased to meet you."

Granddad looked up sharply. "Eh? What's that?"

"You know Zane, Granddad. He brings you to Grace Greenhouse every week."

"Right, right. Are you having a baby?"

Zane stood between her and her mother. At least that meant Mom couldn't see the flush creeping up Kenia's cheeks. "No, Granddad. That's Joanna and Grady. See, she already has a bump where the baby's growing."

The old man looked around, confused.

"Let's have a seat while the girls finish up lunch," Grady interjected.

They'd talked about this ahead of time, deciding Grady might be the best one to keep the situation running smoothly. Kenia hated to think of it as a situation but, other than church, Zane hadn't even seen her parents let alone visited with them. They hadn't exactly gone out of their way for him.

She owed her brother.

A herd of buffalo stampeded around inside Zane's stomach as he took a seat in an overstuffed chair near Clarence and glanced at Grady. He'd never figured he'd get to the *meet the parents* stage of a relationship, especially not with a woman as vibrant and intelligent as Kenia. Intelligent... although she was dating a loser. No, he was going to stop thinking like that. His reading ability — or lack thereof — couldn't define him if he didn't let it.

"Kenia tells me you work over at Retro Village keeping my father and his cronies busy." Barry Akers' words were bland enough, but his gaze was sharp.

"Yes, sir. I'm the activities coordinator there." Zane

grabbed onto Kenia's assumption from long ago. It hadn't been completely wrong. "My grandparents played a major role in my growing-up years, so I've always been comfortable with their generation."

"Always on the go," muttered Clarence. "Nosy visitors all the time, bringing in dogs and cats. Slobbering things."

Zane didn't allow the grin that wanted out. "A lot of the residents miss their pets and enjoy the visits."

Clarence glowered at him.

"But you like the greenhouse trips," Zane reminded him before glancing at Barry. "It's a challenge to find activities for each resident to enjoy. Amos Greenway is a master carpet bowler, and Ida Snyder wouldn't miss knitting class with Mrs. Black for all the tea in China."

Kenia's dad leaned back in his chair and linked his hands behind his head. "I imagine it *is* a challenge, when half of them only want to be left alone. My father was never an extrovert. He preferred puttering with plants to dealing with people. Never really enjoyed the business side of the garden center."

"Makes life more interesting, don't you think?" Grady put in. "If everyone were a businessman, lots of other tasks would be left undone. God created us all different for a purpose."

"Different," muttered Clarence. "Just leave me be."

"The puzzle table is his favorite place," Zane said. "Although, now that flowers are blooming out on the patio, he spends a lot of time out there, too." Not that he was telling the old man's son and grandson anything they didn't know.

Barry eyed him. "What all do you have going on over there, anyway?"

"Well, there's swimming at the YMCA on Thursday and Bingo—"

Clarence jerked in his chair, eyes wide. "Don't let me drown!"

Zane reached over and touched the old man's arm. "No one's making you go to the Y, Clarence. It's only for the residents who *want* to swim." There was also an aquafit class some of them enjoyed, but Clarence wouldn't even know since he'd refused to go after being cajoled the one time.

"Any ideas of activities that might entice him?" Zane glanced between Grady and Barry. "I'm always on the lookout for new ideas, so I'm open to suggestions."

Barry's gaze drilled into him. What was that all about? Chatting with family members about what their elder enjoyed was part of his job. So he wasn't officially on duty, but the topic had come up. Why not pursue it a little? After all, he'd spent a lot of time getting the greenhouse program up and running, but he still needed more ideas, and time was running out. The Village chef had shot down his thoughts on having a few residents help make afternoon snacks occasionally. Trying to start a choir had also hit a sour note.

"Isn't there something going on every day of the week already?" Barry asked.

Zane nodded. "But not every event is well-attended, and a few of the residents haven't found anything that interests them at all."

Grady's chin poked toward his grandfather. "Not all of them are in as good of shape as Granddad, though."

"You're right. Some are in advanced stages of dementia, while others have severe physical limitations."

"I appreciate your attempts to make their last years as comfortable as possible," Barry said.

Zane shifted in his seat. "It's my privilege." Something about the man's words and body language didn't add up, but he couldn't put a finger on it. Yes, he liked the residents, but he didn't love his job. The job he mightn't have much longer. He pushed the thought back under the surface. He was doing his best. If that wasn't good enough, what could he do about it? Even suddenly being able to read fluently wouldn't miraculously give him brilliant ideas to secure the job he wasn't sure he wanted to keep.

Those thoughts only spiraled him downward. He'd become adept at putting on a publicly positive face. That ability would hold him in good stead today as well.

"Where did you grow up, Zane? Where did you go to college?"

Don't panic. Keep smiling. You already know you aren't good enough for this man's daughter.

❧

The ordeal was finally over, and Kenia breathed a sigh of relief as she and Zane made their way to his truck. They'd had a strained, quiet lunch of chilled asparagus soup and sandwiches of sourdough olive bread from A Slice of Heaven. Grady had produced a Greek lemon cake from Demi's Delights and a diamond necklace Kenia had helped pay for. Her mother had declared it a wonderful Mother's Day... and then frowned slightly when she looked at Zane. No one had mentioned Jonah.

Kenia settled into the passenger seat, buckling in as Zane rounded the truck. He started the engine and drove around the circle drive, jaw tense. "Have you called your mom yet?" she asked.

He flicked a glance at her. "No."

"It will make her day."

"I doubt it."

Wait, what? He hadn't talked much about his parents, but of course he needed to phone on Mother's Day. It's what kids, no matter their age, did to honor their moms. Kenia wanted to push it, but maybe not right now. "What did you guys talk about while we were setting lunch out?

"My job."

Uh oh. "Did it... did it go okay? Usually my dad is nicer than my mom."

Zane shrugged and turned onto the street. "I don't think he likes me much."

She reached across the console and rested her hand on his knee. "I'm their baby girl. They're predisposed not to like any man who shows an interest in me."

"You said they liked Jonah."

Oh. Yeah, she'd mentioned that. She shouldn't have. "Jonah and Gloria eloped last week." She shook her head, still in shock. How had his siblings handled missing his wedding?

"How does it make you feel?"

She stared at him. "Jonah finally finding happiness with the woman he loves? I feel fine. I'm happy for him."

"You're sure?"

What was all this about? Kenia pulled her hand away and crossed her arms. "Absolutely certain. Zane, are you okay? What happened in there you haven't told me?"

He glanced at her across the cab. "I like you. A lot."

Whew.

"But I just don't see how this is going to work. Your parents aren't going to give me a break, and they're right. I'm a loser—"

"You're not." Hadn't they been over this? "Zane, you're not. You'll see when we go to Pocatello. The specialist will tell you. She'll give you the tools you need to prove it to yourself and anyone who's doubted you."

"What if she can't help?"

Kenia opened her mouth then snapped it shut. She couldn't make a promise. She didn't know enough about Zane's issues. Arthur Smythe had similar symptoms to Zane's and had been diagnosed with Scotopic Sensitivity Syndrome. That wasn't a guarantee Zane had the same thing. Only the specialist could set his mind at ease... or pull away his newfound, fragile hope.

Lord, give me words. She watched Zane for a long moment. "But what if she can?"

"You're such an optimist."

Yeah, maybe she was, but it was better than wallowing. "I prefer to look on the bright side until all the lights go out."

Zane looked her way with a little grin, shaking his head. "You're good for me."

But was he good for her? Was his depression dragging her down? Maybe it wasn't full-on depression, but she could see the struggle he had every day. Would it always be like this? Was she strong enough for both of them? Would she have to be?

She cared for him — she was afraid to think how much. How would he react if their relationship failed?

It wouldn't. She'd make sure of it. She'd go with him to Pocatello and support him in any way she could. He'd overcome this thing and gain the confidence he needed. Good reading skills would open all the doors for him that he needed. She was certain.

Chapter 18

WOW.

Dozens of men, women, and children, most of whom Zane didn't know, gathered around Evelyn Kujak in front of the main greenhouse, listening to her instructions. Where had the coordinator found so many volunteers? Zane had only come because Kenia informed him this was what they were doing tonight. It seemed a good cause, planting food for the local soup kitchen. He'd doubted there'd be many helpers on hand, no matter what Kenia said.

She nudged his ribs and grinned up at him. "Told you."

He shook his head and chuckled. "I guess I didn't believe you. All those garden beds will be planted in an hour."

"Two at the most. Maisie's got everything organized."

"You mean Evelyn." Maisie was just a kid, not even a teenager yet. Probably a good helper for her mom, though.

"No, I mean Maisie." Kenia's hand swept the area. "This is all Maisie's brainchild. Every bit of it."

"But..."

"She saw an empty lot two years ago. Abandoned greenhouses. She also saw an old, gaunt man with one leg who looked hungry. She saw a woman hanging out in Founders Park at all hours and shared a lunch with her every day. Maisie's the one who put it all together."

Zane looked down at Kenia. She seemed mighty earnest for a liar. "Really?"

"Really. And that's how Evelyn met Ben, when she brought the first load of vegetables to the soup kitchen."

"I had no idea."

"Questions, anyone?" asked Evelyn.

Someone called out for clarification about how much manure to be dug in, and Evelyn answered then asked everyone to form teams beside the long beds.

Kenia dragged Zane to the one nearest the street, where they were joined by a few other people beside a pile of long curved poles.

The kid, Maisie, strutted over. "Your team needs to insert hoops over the walkway between this bed and the one behind it." She jerked her thumb over her shoulder. "See, there are braces for them in the edges of the beds. Then we'll need wire mesh attached to the hoops so the beans will have something to climb. My dad will bring over the roll of wire mesh in a few minutes."

Bossy little kid.

She stuck her thumbs in her shorts pockets and surveyed the adults. "Okay?"

Kenia reached over to high-five the girl. "Good job, Maisie. Putting the hoops over the path instead of the beds themselves is genius."

It was? How?

The kid smirked. "I thought so. Less wasted space, and easier to reach when it's picking time."

Now she was actually taking credit for the design?

"I read a lot of gardening books over the winter. Everything the library had, and Mom even bought me some for Christmas that Mrs. Delis couldn't get through interlibrary loan." The girl looked around with a firm nod. "It's going to be our best garden yet."

Reading. His heart sank. Of course, reading. That's what it always came down to. Those who could make sense of words could do anything. He'd hazard a guess Maisie hadn't bothered with the series from the little kids' section he'd taken out back in March. She was way beyond that.

He would be, too. The kid had a head start on him but, now that he knew words didn't dance for everyone else, he'd figure out how to make them hold still for him. The specialist would help. Arthur would help. He cast a sidelong glance at Kenia. She seemed willing to help, too.

"Kenia!" A pretty woman with long auburn hair reached out for a hug. "I haven't seen you in ages."

"Hi, Serena! I didn't expect you to be here. How's the movie coming?"

Movie? Zane looked from the woman to the dark-haired man behind her. Wasn't that the guy from the bakery? But not Jonah.

Serena wrinkled her nose. "Forever on hold, it seems. So I'm back to making pottery when Micah's at work." She eyed Zane, her eyebrows tilting slightly upward.

"I'd like you two to meet my friend Zane Russell. Zane, this is Serena and Micah Baxter." Kenia smiled at her friend. "Serena used to star in that teenage ninja series my friends and I were addicted to way back when. Serena VanDerLay."

"Pleased to meet you." He nodded to the couple.

Awkward. Not only had he had a crush on the hot teen star like most of his buddies, he'd been introduced to her merely as Kenia's friend, not boyfriend. What was going on? Was she embarrassed of him, after all?

"Zane?" Micah pointed toward the pile of hoops. "Those look heavy. Want to give me a hand bringing them over? The girls can bolt them to the wooden frames."

"Uh, sure." He spent the next half hour at the other

end of the eight-foot hoops from the brother of Kenia's former boyfriend being bossed around by a preteen while his girlfriend ignored him as she chatted with a movie star. Not quite what he'd expected when he agreed to join the workday.

Oh, come on, Russell. Put some muscle to it and quit sulking. But he hadn't been sulking. Not really. Just trying to figure out how life had gotten so weird.

Micah looked around. "Anyone seen Ben? He was going to bring over the mesh."

Serena pointed. "Isn't that him fixing the tomato supports over there?"

"Looks like he's busy," Zane put in. "I know where they keep the rolls in that shed over there. Give me a hand?" He looked at Micah. "We can take a load off Ben."

"Sure thing."

"Kenia looks happy." Micah glanced at him as they strode toward the shed. "I'm glad to see it. She's a good person."

"She is."

The other guy grinned. "Been going out with her long?"

"A few weeks." A bit of pride swelled in Zane's chest. "She's kind of amazing."

"You've got it bad." Micah chuckled. "Be good to her."

Zane pulled open the shed door and blinked against the sudden darkness. "I will. That's the roll over there."

"Got it."

⟋⟋

"Whew." Kenia stripped off her work gloves and wiped sweat off her forehead. She was probably leaving a smear of dirt in its wake, but whatever. "That was a long day. My muscles won't be speaking to me tomorrow. Or, rather, they'll be screaming."

Zane offered that lopsided grin she loved so much as he stepped in behind her. His strong hands rested on her shoulders as his thumbs dug into the knots.

"Ooooh. That kills." She leaned into his touch.

He eased up slightly but kept massaging. Around them, other weary workers headed for their cars, leaving behind a dozen long raised beds filled with assorted green plants.

Kenia closed her eyes, listening to the fading voices and departing vehicles while absorbing Zane's touch. Wouldn't it be nice if this could go on forever? But, all too soon, his hands slid around her waist and his face nuzzled into her shoulder. She sighed. "Thanks. That felt great."

He kissed the curve of her neck. "We should grab our swimsuits and go down to the swimming hole."

She shivered, a combination of the thought of cold

water and what his lips were doing. "I was thinking more of a long hot bubble bath and a good book." She could see it now. A few candles on the deck of her tub, quiet music.

"I can't join you for that."

A giggle burbled out. "So true." Not yet, anyway. He'd seemed aloof today — ever since Mother's Day at her parents' house, really — but today had been for planting the gardens for Corinna's Cupboard, not for mooning over each other.

"Or we could grab takeout and drive down to Miracle Hot Springs. It's only a half hour or so. That's if you're looking for hot water instead of cold." He nibbled her ear.

Oh, man. "I wish I could. I'm meeting Matt Gonzalez tonight to go over the construction plans for the building."

Zane shifted away, and the air chilled. "I didn't know you were hiring him. Drew's too busy?"

Kenia turned to face him and wrinkled her nose. "You were right. He's booking for next spring now, and I can't wait that long."

"Matt doesn't have as good a reputation as Drew."

"I know, but it's a fairly straightforward job. Breaking out three windows that someone bricked up a few decades back. Then two arches between the two halves. We can't open the whole thing up because—"

"Because it's a load bearing wall. It's not *that*

straightforward."

"Right. That's what Drew said. Matt figures we could cut bigger openings than Drew did, though."

Zane's eyebrows pulled together. "Do you *need* bigger openings? Because I'd trust Drew's opinion over Matt's any day of the week."

"I hear you, but Matt has some good ideas." She glanced at her watch. "I need to get rolling if I'm going to fit that bubble bath in first. See you at church in the morning?"

Indecision seemed to dance in Zane's eyes. "Want me to come to your meeting tonight?"

He really didn't trust Matt, did he? "No, it's okay. It's my store, so I have to figure it out. I'm sure you have things to do, anyway." Too late, she remembered the invitation to the hot springs. He wouldn't have offered that if he had other plans.

"Nothing more important than you." He backed up a step. "But, I get it."

Kenia reached out and caught his arm. "It's not like that. I know you have some renovation experience."

His eyebrows hiked.

Okay, Zane had done a marvelous job on his house. The guy should be a contractor in his own right, but he wasn't. He wasn't set up for permits with town hall and didn't have a list of electricians and plumbers to call. It wasn't like she could hire him to do the work.

She was bungling this, and he was obviously

frustrated. How could she smooth things over without backpedaling? Because regardless of where their relationship ended up, Page Turners was hers. It was her money on the line. Well, hers, Dad's, and the bank's, but she was solely responsible for the outcome. She had to trust her instincts. Couldn't let Zane unsettle her and make her second-guess herself.

"Hope your meeting goes well." Zane backed up a few more steps, his expression closed off. "I'll see you around."

"Church tomorrow?"

He shrugged. "Maybe. I have some stuff to do so I can take Wednesday off for Pocatello."

"Pick me up at eight? Or do we want to take my car? It's cheaper on fuel."

"You still want to come?"

What on earth was wrong with him? "Yes, of course I do. I'm looking forward to it. To spending the day with you. To being there when you get answers."

"There might not be any answers."

Maybe worry caused him to be prickly. Made sense. "I'm sure there will be."

"You can't guarantee that."

"No, I can't. But that's what I'm praying for. Answers and miracles."

Zane shook his head. "There aren't any miracles, Kenia. I've been praying for those my entire life. If they existed, surely God would have sent them by now."

She had no answers, but she could offer comfort. And she definitely needed to be at his side on Wednesday. Kenia stepped forward and wrapped her arms around him, but he didn't reciprocate. Too bad she couldn't put Matt off, but she needed to nail down the plans so he could start in August. "I'll give you a call after the meeting."

Zane's jaw clenched. "If you want to."

"Of course, I do." She stretched and swept a kiss over his lips.

He pushed her gently away, his gaze lingering as he did so. Then he turned and strode toward his truck, leaving her standing there.

Kenia stared after him as he drove away then became aware of someone beside her.

"Everything okay?" asked Evelyn. "Or is there trouble in paradise?"

Kenia shook her head. "I wish I knew. Why do men have to be so difficult to understand?"

Her friend laughed. "I think I've heard Ben say the exact same thing about women."

"Probably. But I don't know how to take him half the time. He has some issues — who doesn't? — but he gets so moody sometimes. Like now. I have no clue what I said wrong." Okay, she had a vague clue. What did he expect her to do? Wait a year for Drew Harrison? She couldn't. She had to deal with whomever was available.

Evelyn slung her arm over Kenia's shoulder. "Better to work through those things now, before you're too far in. This is different than with Jonah, isn't it?"

"Night and day different. I liked Jonah a lot. Still do. I mean, what's not to like? But he never made my heart sing the way Zane does."

"You're in love."

Was she? "I don't know how to tell. I thought that was coming with Jonah, that a slow start with friendship at the center was best, but I was wrong."

"No, you weren't. That's a great way for love to start, but it isn't a guarantee, and it isn't the only way it arrives."

Kenia glanced at her friend. "Married only a year and a half and now you're an expert?" She grinned to soften the words.

"Joanna and Grady were at each other's throats at the beginning. Alaina and Cameron fell in love in minutes, practically, but had big things to overcome. And Ben was more like Zane, with struggles in his past that made it hard for him to open up." Evelyn wrinkled her nose. "Not that I didn't have issues of my own."

"So what do you think are my issues?"

"Hmm. Do you really want to know?"

Kenia laughed. "Sure, why not?"

"Well, you're outgoing. You're certain everyone in the world would be your friend if they only knew you."

"That's an issue?"

"Only for someone who finds it harder to trust people, who prefers the shadows."

"I guess. What else?"

"You're independent."

"I fail to see the problem here. I'm an Akers, after all."

"I get it, though I wasn't raised to it like you were. I was forced into it when I was pregnant with Maisie. Men like to protect the women they love, though. I had a hard time letting Ben in close enough to lean on him, but it goes both ways."

"Hmm. So that's why Zane's so bristly."

Evelyn raised her eyebrows.

"I'm making big decisions these days about the retail building. Revisioning the space. Hiring a contractor." And she'd turned Zane away when he wanted to be part of it. She'd thought he wouldn't want to spend time surrounded by books. After all, he rarely entered Page Turners and always looked uncomfortable when he did.

"Ask his advice?"

Kenia groaned. "He already gave it, unsolicited. And I rejected it." Knowing didn't change anything, though. She still needed a contractor, she needed him in August, and Drew wasn't available. What was she going to do?

Chapter 19

ZANE COULD HARDLY WAIT until they were back out onto the sidewalk before giving Kenia a whirl. "Oh, man! Can you believe it?"

She beamed at him. "I'm so thrilled for you."

Thrilled barely touched what he felt. After dozens of overlays in dozens of colors, shades, and hues all of a sudden the page had stood still. All the words lined up in neat rows like soldiers at attention rather than like rowdy schoolboys when classes let out for the summer. The words stood still! He'd barely allowed himself to dream of the possibility.

Zane covered Kenia's mouth with his own and kissed her with all the pent-up emotions he could finally release. He kissed her until he could barely stand up and, by the sway of her in his arms, she felt the same.

He leaned his forehead against hers. "I can read." He heard the wonder in his own voice.

She giggled. "There's only one thing that could make this even better."

Better? How could anything on the planet improve the outcome? Maybe asking her to marry him. Well, no. Not now. Not today, but suddenly the idea didn't fill him with terror. Anything was possible now... or would be upon the arrival of his new glasses, infused with the exact hue of blue-gray that snapped his brain into focus.

"That's crazy talk, woman. This is the pinnacle of my experience. Or one of them, at least. You are the other." He brushed his lips across hers then went in for a deeper kiss.

When he released her, her eyes twinkled as she looked up at him, even while she gasped for air.

"Out with it," he growled. "What could make this better?"

She leaned back in his arms with hers entwined around his neck. "She sure had a lot of colors there. Everything I could imagine."

He nodded, eyebrows raised. Yellows, pinks, purples, greens — the array of shades and hues had indeed seemed endless.

"I thought it would be fun if your brain worked well with pink. Then I could tell everyone you were looking at life through rose-tinted glasses."

A laugh erupted from deep within him. "Lucky escape for me, then. Bad enough getting used to wearing glasses after a lifetime of perfect vision."

"But it will be worth it."

"Oh, darling, you've got that right. To read like a normal person. I can't believe it was so simple."

"Simple, but not something we'd ever have thought of."

Zane shook his head. "I thought I'd been there, done that, with vision therapy back in school. If only they'd known their tests were so incomplete..."

"You'd have been spared half your life of worry."

He met her sympathetic gaze. "Yeah. I'd have finished high school. Maybe gone to college."

"You still could, if you wanted."

He could, couldn't he? He felt like he'd lived in a cramped, dark tunnel that had finally opened up to a vast vista. Like existing inside the lava tube caves at Craters of the Moon National Monument before discovering the unending Idaho plains and skies just outside. He shook his head in wonder.

"Really, you could. What would you like to do with your life? It's all open, Zane. Doctor, lawyer..."

He shuddered. "Please, no. That many years of school still sounds like punishment."

"You're smart. You'd probably find it easy now."

"Not interested." His parents would push hard, though. That is, if this turn of events piqued their interest in him again. If he bothered to tell them. He sure wouldn't until he had the glasses and had been wearing them long enough to be certain they made the difference. He hadn't jumped to conclusions in that diagnostician's office, had he? Wanted so much for the concept to be reality he'd imagined it so?

No, Kenia had been there. She'd heard the results with her own ears, seen them with her own eyes. It was real.

He opened the car door for her then rounded the vehicle and slid in himself. "Where to for lunch?"

Being here with Zane, seeing the wonder — the hope — in his eyes was one of the best days of her life. Someone had rolled a huge weight off his chest turning him into the fun-loving man she'd only had intriguing glimpses of before. They fed the ducks, tried on goofy hats in a boutique, and raced across the park, holding hands and laughing into the wind.

And, oh, the kisses. There was hope in them, too. A promise of more to come. Kenia's visions pushed to the forefront, those glimpses of her and Zane and a few adorable babies with his dark hair, enticing dimple, and startling brown eyes. When he was moody, she'd pushed those idyllic thoughts away, trying to remember how unpleasant it might be to live with someone who had such a struggle going on within, but today? With the sun shining down on them? The dreams grew wings of their own until she could almost see him waiting for her at the front of Grace Fellowship for their fairy tale wedding.

Kenia let out a happy sigh and felt Zane's arm around her waist tighten as they strolled back toward her car. She tucked her thumb through his belt loop and leaned against his shoulder.

He kissed her hair. "Good day?"

"The best." She nudged him with her hip. "I'll never forget the look of wonder on your face when she slid that overlay across the text. A thrill ran through me from the top of my head to the soles of my feet."

"I didn't see your hair stand on end."

She laughed. "Trust me, it tried, but there's too much product in it."

"And then she took it away."

"But only to replace it with a different one. It might've been even better. Even clearer."

Zane shook his head. "Not remotely possible. I felt like she'd purged all oxygen from the planet. I wanted to grab her hand and put that thing back. Glue it in place."

"Oh, now you wanted to grab *her* hand?" Kenia tickled his ribs. "She's the age of my mother and wearing diamonds on her left hand that cost a king's fortune. Definitely taken."

He caught her hand and pulled it away from his side. "Your mother's are bigger." The teasing slipped from his voice.

Kenia chuckled. "Dad adds to her rings on every fifth anniversary. I hate to see what he'll come up with for their fortieth next year. They're already taking up her whole left hand."

Silence. And the touch on her waist fell away.

She looked up at him, at the mask that slid right back over his face. His eyes stared off into the distance, and his lips pursed slightly. "Zane?" She turned on the sidewalk and set her hands on both his hips.

Hands still at his sides, he glanced at her then focused just beyond her ear.

What had just happened? She had a pretty good guess, but it seemed presumptuous to mention it. Still, she already desperately missed the carefree Zane of the past few hours. "I'm not my mother," she said softly. "I don't measure love by how many carats are in a diamond."

Zane caught her right hand and lifted it between them.

Glistening in the sunlight, the circle of tiny diamonds drew attention to the gleaming peridot in her birthstone ring. He'd seen it before, that first day he'd come into the bookstore. His birthday was in November. Topaz.

"Your parents have a lot of money."

She nodded. It was only a fact, after all.

"I... I care for you a lot, Kenia, but I can't compete with that. I'm an activities coordinator at a nursing home. I'll never make the kind of money that can give

217

you what you're accustomed to."

And he might soon be out of a job. "But with the new glasses, you have every opportunity in the world. You can *read* now. You can be anything you want to be. Do anything."

"So my current job isn't good enough?"

What on earth? Her eyebrows furrowed as she looked up at him. "I don't think that's what I said. I wouldn't have dated you at all if I were that shallow."

"Then why are you pushing me?" His thumb rubbed across the peridot.

"I didn't think I was. You're good with Granddad and his buddies. You're good with the kids at Grace Greenhouse. You did a gorgeous job renovating your house. You have so many talents. I only wish to encourage you to dream big, now that your horizons have opened up."

His dark eyes zeroed in on hers, unreadable. "You dreamed big, buying not only the bookstore but the commercial space it's in."

He did understand, after all. "Exactly."

"With your father's money."

She'd like to refute that, but couldn't. "He's invested some into it, that's true. But I also have a bank loan. It's up to me to make the right decisions and prove out my ideas. I could lose it all."

Zane laughed, but not with mirth. "Daddy wouldn't let you fail."

Would he? Probably not. But still, how had they got here in the conversation? A few minutes ago they hadn't had a care in the world, and now he was throwing her father's wealth at her? It wasn't like he hadn't known who her parents were all along. If it was going to be a problem, why hadn't it come up sooner?

"I don't have that kind of safety net, Kenia. My parents have money, too, but I can assure you they wouldn't come running to bail me out if I overstretched and got into trouble. Sure, I have the house, and I'm thankful for it. It's not every day a guy with a dead-end job owns his own home, free and clear."

"I'm happy for you." What else could she say?

"Today has given me hope I might be able to get a better job, but I'm not certain, and it will take some time to make up for lost time. Plus, I don't know for sure those glasses will help that much. I don't want to count on it. Not yet."

She wanted to tell him to grab his dreams and run like they'd just dashed across the park, hand in hand. To feel the exhilaration of it all, and get up again if he stumbled. But, somehow, her lips stayed zipped.

"Opportunities are not unlimited in a town the size of Arcadia Valley," he said.

"Lots of people commute to Twin Falls. It's not that far, really. Not if you find a job there you love." A sudden thought struck her. "Dad's greenhouse manager will be retiring in a few years. He — or I mean Grady

— would probably hire you if you wanted to get your degree in horticulture."

"Kenia, stop. I don't want a pity position."

It wouldn't be one. He'd be qualified. Of course, that would mean four years away in Salt Lake City or Boise or even farther afield while Kenia was tied to Arcadia Valley. She couldn't just up and leave her brand-new business to be with Zane while he went to college. "Never mind. It was a terrible idea anyway."

"Maybe staying at Retro Village wouldn't be so bad. If I can read better, I'll be able to do a better job. Maybe even get a promotion."

Uh... no. "Mr. Davis's job is the only one directly upline from yours, isn't it?"

Zane nodded. "I guess."

"He's like in his early fifties, so he's probably not going anywhere anytime soon. The board combed far and wide to find him when the previous director retired. They were looking for someone who had some experience, and he'd worked his way to second in command at a large care facility in Provost."

"How do you know so much about him?" Zane's eyebrows peaked. "How long has your grandfather been at Retro, anyway?"

"Um... under three years." And Mr. Davis had been there much longer. Kenia should've kept her mouth shut. "Did you want to catch supper here before we head home, or what?" Too late she remembered Zane had mentioned putting stew in his slow cooker. He'd invited her. Oh, man. She was taking her foot out of her mouth only to insert the other one.

He searched her face. Why wasn't *now* the time he'd stare at something on the horizon instead? "I made dinner for us already."

She smiled. "Sorry, I forgot. I'm sure it will be great."

"About Retro. You were right when you said something about me working there because of my bond with my grandparents. I'm sure that made the thought of spending all day with the elderly into something normal. Maybe now that I can read and research easily — or at least, I hope I'll be able to — I'll be able to find more activities for the residents to do that they really enjoy."

Did he know, or didn't he? Was he protecting her from the knowledge of his impending job loss? They'd brainstormed ideas together, but he'd always framed it as what would Granddad enjoy, not as something to save his job. Kenia was the one who strolled around life with rose-colored glasses, but she was fresh out of ideas for activities. Too many of the seniors were like Granddad and only wanted to do one or two things, grumbling at the rest of the offerings. "But what if you can't?"

"What if I can't *what*?"

She'd let the zipper loose on her mouth. "If you can't

find enough activities to make Mr. Davis happy soon enough."

His eyes narrowed. "How do you know what Mr. Davis said?"

Uh oh. "Didn't you say something...?"

Zane shook his head. "Pretty sure I haven't, no."

She stared into those stormy eyes, wracking her brain for a conversation that might've hinted to what she already knew. Came up empty. She sucked in her lip.

"Kenia. Tell me."

There was no way to pass this off as nothing important. Not with the intensity in his gaze, his absolute focus. "I know that's how Retro works with non-regulatory positions."

His eyebrows rose as he waited for her to continue.

"Dad might be on the board of directors."

Zane swung away, the line of his mouth grim. "Of course."

She grabbed for his hand and missed. "I thought you knew." Even to her, that sounded lame.

He took a step back. "How could I know?"

"Well, it's not exactly secret information. The list of directors is on the website. Probably on a plaque on the wall somewhere."

"I couldn't read, remember? You think I'd just randomly surf the internet on the off chance I might discover your father's name connected to Retro?"

"When you put it that way, no. Look, I'm sorry,

Zane. He probably shouldn't have said anything to me about the review."

"You're darn right he shouldn't have. So all this time you're just feeling sorry for me, trying to help me keep my job? That stings, Kenia. That really stings."

"How could you think that? That's so unfair. I feel a lot of things for you, and sorry isn't one of them."

"Oh?" But the tone of his voice was hard.

Kenia gulped. "I think... I think I might love you. That's definitely not the same thing as pity."

"Love?" He laughed. "Am I your rebellious phase then, to go against Daddy's wishes? Or did he put you up to it so that your grandfather would have all the benefits of a well-rounded social life?"

She'd laid her heart out for Zane, and this was his response? Tears threatened to flood her eyes, but she blinked them back and kept her chin steady. "If you think that, you're truly delusional. Have you already forgotten all the good times we've had? If you think I'd kiss just anyone that way, you're dead wrong."

"You were on the rebound."

Kenia gritted her teeth. "I was *not* on the rebound. I did need a bit of time to recover from Jonah's rejection, that's true." She couldn't lose Zane the same way. There'd be no recovery from him, not if she lived as long as Granddad. "But he hurt my pride more than—"

"The Akers' pride."

"Would you stop it? Forget about my parents. They

do not rule my decisions or dictate my love life."
Although they'd tried, with Jonah. Mom, especially.

"Kenia, I..."

She stared at him, chin up. She'd said the L word. If he didn't reciprocate those feelings, it would be Jonah all over again. Her jumping to conclusions. Too hopeful. Instead, she'd wind up like Aunt Irene, living out her days in the apartment above Page Turners.

Alone.

Chapter 20

ANE TOOK THE GLASSES OFF. Put them back on. Off. On. It was like playing frozen tag. Words in Quinn's adventure magazine ran. Then stood still.

Where had these things been all his life? Too bad they weren't really rose-colored, since they were the only bright spot in a world that had otherwise narrowed to a dull blue-grey without Kenia in it.

How had he been so stupid that day in Pocatello? He'd been so raw, unprepared for all the emotions that came with his vision clicking into focus. He didn't deal with emotions. Ever. Just shoved them into a black hole and slammed on the lid. But the lid hadn't held tight with all that bubbling hope, and the whole top had blown off, letting loose the good, the bad, and the ugly. Mostly the ugly.

I think... I think I might love you.

Kenia's words. With all those emotions roiling around, he hadn't known how to respond. Instead of gathering her in his arms and admitting he loved her, too, he'd thrown that lid back on. Two weeks later, it was apparent he was a fool.

He'd seen her Tuesdays at the greenhouse, always busy with Clarence or Ida or the twins. Never meeting his gaze. Never letting her wild crazy laughter tumble free.

"Bro. Thought those glasses would bring a smile to your face."

Zane looked up to see Tony standing across the table. "They're great. I can't tell you what a huge difference."

Tony lifted a stack of paperbacks. "I stopped by Page Turners and picked up a new series to read."

Zane's heart hiccupped. "Thought you preferred e-books."

"Mostly I do." Tony parked them on the table. "But I needed an excuse to stop by and talk to Kenia."

Asking her out already? Thanks, man.

"Since you refuse to talk about what happened, I thought I'd try her."

"Oh."

"Russell, she's in the storefront next door taking out a wall with a sledgehammer. Trying to convince me her bloodshot eyes are from the dust she's creating."

A sledgehammer? Bloodshot eyes?

"And she's just as talkative as you." Tony raised an

eyebrow. "Would you two get over this already, whatever it is? You're miserable, and she's no better. I never thought I'd see the day when all that girl had were short, monotone responses. Not Kenia, the life of the party."

Zane had done that to her. He'd mocked her declaration of love. How could he have? She was the best thing that had ever happened to him. Better even than these stupid glasses. What good were words, reading, without the woman from the bookstore? He swallowed the lump in his throat. "Everything I touch turns sour."

His housemate pivoted a chair around and straddled it. "So not true."

Sure it was. His relationship with his parents. Flunking out of school. Dead-end job after dead-end job, this one with a performance review coming in a couple of weeks that he was going to fail as well. He had a history of leaving disaster in his wake.

"Listen to me. Why do you think Jesus came to earth?"

Zane blinked. Where was this coming from? But it was an easy answer. "To save us. Give us eternal life."

"Save us from what?"

"Our sin." Add his devotional life to the list of things that had gone south recently.

"To give us a hope and a future. Not so we stay stuck in the ruts we're in. So that we can embrace the abundant life He has planned for us."

"We reap what we sow." He'd planted a mess, over and over, and that's what he deserved to harvest.

"Russell." Tony rolled his eyes. "That's the cycle Jesus came to break. Sure, we're sinners. We deserve death. Paul said that in Romans: 'the wages of sin is death, but Jesus came to give us eternal life.' The natural order was broken."

"I know that, man." Zane jerked to his feet.

"Do you?" Tony tilted his head and looked up at him. "Because you're acting like you're stuck. You've heard how they train elephants, right?"

How... who... *what*?

"The handlers tie the baby elephant's leg to something firm so they can't go anywhere. When they're full-grown, that cord couldn't possibly hold them if they just walked away. But they don't go anywhere, because their mind is what's trapped. They think they're secured with unbreakable chains. They're not."

Zane's mind reeled. Was he only stuck because he thought he was? Mind games. Bah.

Tony grabbed the books off the table as he rose. "Think about it. The whole premise of the Bible, of Christianity, is that we don't *have* to reap what we've sown. Jesus came to alter that. Praying for you, bro." He sauntered into the living room, settled into his favorite easy chair, and opened one of the paperbacks.

Consequences were *not* inevitable? Zane sank back into his chair and cradled his head in his hands. Why had he forgotten what his faith was all about? Chains broken. The past gone. If anyone knew, it would have been the apostle Paul. He'd been killing Christians before God stopped him in his tracks. The man had certainly planted disaster after disaster, but when he'd seen Jesus for who He really was — the Son of the living God — he'd repented and started down a new path, one where his consequences didn't match his previous actions.

Why was Zane living as though the outcome was inevitable? Sure, he'd planted lots of junk of his own, but he didn't have to pick the fruit of it. He could harvest hope. Love.

I came that they may have life... and have it abundantly.

Jesus' words in John chapter ten. Zane closed his eyes. "Lord, why didn't I see it before? You didn't just save me *from* sin. You saved me *for* abundant life."

"You look terrible."

Kenia eyed her friend across the white tablecloth in L'Aubergine. "Thanks, but I didn't come here to be insulted."

"Not sleeping these days?" Alaina asked.

"Allergies."

"To what? Not books, I hope."

"Dust, apparently. I decided to take out the wall in the other half of the building myself."

Alaina reached across and touched Kenia's hand. "I'm sorry. I didn't realize your budget was that tight."

"It's not." Kenia took a sip of her coffee. Caffeinated. Decaffeinated. She wasn't sleeping either way, and it was doubtful that herbal tea like in her friend's cup would make any difference.

"Then why?"

She sighed. "Sometimes a person just needs to smash things, you know? I never took karate when I was a kid, so I figured a sledgehammer would be a better bet than trying with my bare hands."

"You're not making this easy." Her friend grinned. "Tell me what violence is the answer to."

The waitress set two pieces of cheesecake in front of them. "Can I get you anything else?"

"We're good, thanks." Alaina smiled up at her then pointed a narrowed stare across the table. "Talk."

Kenia took a bite of her dessert. "Jonah makes the best cheesecake. I can't believe he's still working two jobs."

"We did *not* come here to talk about Jonah." Alaina rolled her eyes. "But the fact that you brought him up confirms the fact that something's gone wrong with Zane. I've seen you two avoiding each other at the greenhouse like someone has an infectious disease."

"I think I'll be like my aunt and spend my life alone. The bookstore, church, family, friends... that will be enough for me."

"Or you could take the sledgehammer to Zane's thick skull and ram some sense into him."

Mouth open, Kenia stared at her friend. "You did not just say that."

"Well, I finally got your attention. Trust me, with two bloodthirsty almost eight-year-olds, there's a lot of deconstruction in our house. It might not be safe for the—" Alaina tightened her lips.

"For the what?"

"Nothing. I was just saying I understand why violence might seem like the answer. It does to Evan, every day."

"For the baby. You're pregnant." Kenia's heart sank. She wanted to be happy for Alaina and Cameron. For Grady and Joanna. But today, when it seemed likely that she'd never have the experience of giving birth herself, let alone be blissfully married to the man of her dreams — who was definitely Zane Russell, not Jonah Baxter — eager joy was hard to muster.

"Yeah." Alaina toyed with her chamomile tea. "I didn't mean to tell anyone yet. We're due early January."

"Congratulations!" There'd been good enthusiasm in that, right?

"Thanks. Please don't tell. I've had some spotting, and we're not sure everything will be all right."

"I'll pray for you." Kenia squeezed her friend's hand. Like her prayers would do any good. She'd prayed fervently, every single day since that trip to Pocatello and, as far as she could tell, God wasn't answering. Her only hope lay in Jesus' story about the midnight visitor. The man didn't get up to help his neighbor because they were friends. Not at all. He went to the door because his neighbor kept on pounding on it and begging for help.

And I tell you, ask, and it will be given to you, Jesus said about the story. *Seek, and you will find; knock, and it will be opened to you. For everyone who asks receives, and the one who seeks finds, and to the one who knocks it will be opened.*

So she kept knocking, but the door wasn't opening. Did God want her to reach out and test the knob? She'd been battling with that question as she destroyed the unneeded walls in the other storefront.

"Okay, so you know my secret. What happened with Zane?"

Kenia sighed. "Ever since I've known him, he's oscillated between impulsive and fun-loving... and kind of depressed. He's hard to read." What an understatement.

"I've noticed he's a bit moody, but that improved a lot over the past couple of months."

Should she spill Zane's secret? But soon he'd be

wearing colored lenses in public, and the truth was sure to come out. "Turns out he had good reason."

Alaina's hand squeezed hers. "Not a brain tumor..."

"What? No. Nothing like that at all."

"I'm so glad. I've been worried."

"No, something much simpler." Kenia ate a bite of the cheesecake then met her friend's concerned gaze. "He has Scotopic Sensitivity Syndrome."

Alaina blinked. "He has *what*?"

"It's a problem with the brain's ability to process visual information. It's like there's a disconnect in there."

"I don't understand."

Here went nothing. "Zane can't read." When her friend's eyes widened and her mouth formed an 'o,' Kenia went on. "I've seen some mockups of what he sees. Words on the page jump and jiggle and change places while he struggles to make sense of them."

"Seriously? That's a thing? It sounds super annoying."

"Yeah. It's a thing. Turns out I even had a couple of books about it in Page Turners but didn't connect the dots. *Reading by the Colors* by Helen Irlen is one of them. It really opened my eyes to what Zane's been going through." She leaned forward. "He's been fighting with this alone his entire life. He had some testing done when he was a kid but they missed this. He figured either everyone else was faking their ability to read, or he was a weird anomaly. He was embarrassed and kept it hidden."

"Oh, man. No wonder..." Alaina shook her head. "Wow. But he told you?"

"Only because he made one last attempt to figure it all out and met a volunteer adult literary coach down at the library. Arthur Smythe has had the same struggles and connected Zane with a diagnostician." Kenia toyed with her mug. "We went to Pocatello two weeks ago to meet with her."

"And it was bad news."

She shook her head. "It was fabulous news. With the right shade of lenses — it sounds weird, but it works. I totally saw it for myself — those words hold still, and he can read."

Alaina leaned forward. "That's great, really. But I don't get it. It's about two weeks ago since the two of you went into this deep funk. If he had such great news, I'd think you guys would be on cloud nine."

A bitter chuckled escaped. "Reasonable assumption. But I opened my big mouth and tried to get him to dream big. To think about college and what he wanted to do with his life. His job at Retro is dead-end."

Alaina's eyebrows went up. "You tried to change who he is."

"Well, not exactly. But I let something slip I shouldn't have known in the first place." Should she be telling Alaina this? "Dad's on the board of directors for

Retro, and so I knew they might be letting Zane go. Budget cuts."

Her friend grimaced.

"I was only trying to help, but he took it all wrong and threw the Akers' money in my face, like he wasn't good enough for me the way he is. He didn't know my dad was on the board. It's not like it's some big secret, but Zane doesn't read, so he hadn't figured it out. Anyway, I told him I loved him, and he decided I was just trying to get back at my father. Driving back from Pocatello was the longest two hours of my life." And a memory she couldn't diminish no matter how her muscles ached from swinging a sledgehammer.

"You love him?"

Kenia stabbed at her cheesecake. "Yeah."

"Did you love Jonah?"

She shook her head. "I hoped we'd get there, but no. I liked him a lot. But Zane makes my heart beat faster, and his kisses are out of this world." She met Alaina's gaze. "Not just that. I think he makes me a better person. I know he loves the Lord. He's shared with me stuff he's learned from the devotional app he uses that reads Scripture to him."

"Have you tried to talk to him?"

"By text. By email. By voicemail. No response."

"By camping out on his doorstep?"

"That seems creepy."

"Desperate times call for desperate measures."

Maybe her friend was right.

"Let me think." Alaina angled her head and tapped a finger to her chin. "Are you busy Saturday morning?"

"I have to work. Why?"

"Can you get out of it? Because I have an idea."

Kenia squinted at her friend. Anything to break the impasse. "I can ask Aunt Irene. She's usually flexible." Add hiring an employee or two to her to-do list.

"Good. I'll get back to you."

Chapter 21

A WKWARD. ZANE SAT TOWARD the end of the table at the Sunrise with a bunch of men he barely knew. Okay, he knew Tony. And Cameron and Grady, which was even more weird since they were on Team Kenia. When the Baxter twins walked in, signing to each other, Zane choked back a groan, but at least Jonah wasn't on their heels.

No. Zane lived in Arcadia Valley and had no intention of moving out. He really liked Pastor Ivan's sermons, the music, and the upbeat feel at Grace Fellowship. He'd get over this discomfort with Kenia eventually — he'd have to — but he wasn't going anywhere. These men could still be his friends. Right? Well, maybe not Grady or Cameron. But some of them.

When the waitress had taken their order and closed the door to the private back room, Corban DeWitt opened his Bible. "My turn today, guys. I'd like to be more prepared, but Andrew is waking up like every two hours all night, and I'm bushed." The DeWitts' baby had been born prematurely but had been home now for a couple of months.

A few of the men murmured in sympathy.

"One of the songs that keeps coming up in my playlist is *Strong Enough* by Matthew West. You guys heard it?" Corban poked at his phone. "I want to play it for you, because it is totally where I'm coming from these past few months."

Zane listened as the artist sang of needing God's hands of mercy covering him because he wasn't strong enough to be or do what he needed to on his own. Maybe that was the point, the lyrics went on. A guy didn't start looking up until he was at rock bottom, after all.

"Sometimes things come up that really show us we're not strong enough on our own." Corban grinned, shaking his head. "Not what macho men want to hear, is it?"

Cameron chuckled. "Not so much."

"But that's when we have to let go and let God, as the saying goes. Philippians 4:13 says, 'I can do all things through Him who strengthens me.' I know you guys all know that, but sometimes we need a reminder. When I was praying about what to share today, I kept coming back to this." Corban looked straight at Zane. "Someone here needs to hear these words."

Zane shifted, the wooden chair suddenly un-comfortable. But then Corban's gaze focused on Tony for a long second before switching to Micah. Okay, he hadn't been singled out. But his heart said he might as well have been. That song had summed up his entire life. He'd never been strong enough or good enough, no matter what he did. The new glasses, in their case in his chest pocket, made a difference in some areas, but not to his feeling of self-worth.

Tony's words from the other day trickled through his mind. He didn't have to reap what he'd sown. Jesus had come to give him hope and a future... but was that future with Kenia? Too much time had passed now. He was going to look like a fool going back to her and apologizing. Wasn't that how the saying went? *It's better to be thought a fool than to open one's mouth and remove all doubt.*

But what if she forgave him? Wouldn't that be worth all the humbling in the world?

Corban looked around the table. "Anyone have any prayer requests today? Remember whatever is shared in this room is always completely confidential." He grimaced. "Please pray for Andrew. I know this is how babies are, but Ruth and I could sure use some sleep."

"For our adoption process," Micah said. "I know the whole process could take years, but prayer can't hurt, right? Somewhere out there is a baby who needs us." He grinned at Corban. "Serena and I would like to join you on the sleepless nights."

The men laughed.

"Please pray for one of the homeless women who comes to Corinna's Cupboard," put in Ben. "Rona is having some health issues."

"I'd like prayers for wisdom," said Tony. "I've started looking at options for my restaurant in Spokane, and I really need God's guidance."

One after the other, the men laid out prayer requests. How could they trust each other so completely? Zane had never had anyone to call friend like this in his entire life. He hadn't even known he longed for it until today. Until Tony's repeated invitations to the men's group had finally worn him down.

Corban checked his watch. "We've got ten minutes before they bring in breakfast. Any other prayer requests? Then let's get to it."

Should he? Why not? Zane lifted his hand. "I have one."

"Go ahead."

"I've got a job review coming up next week, and I'm not sure what the outcome will be. I could use prayer for peace." He shifted in his seat, stifling a chuckle. Man, that must've sounded awkward. "Maybe prayer for new opportunities."

"You've got it." Corban closed his eyes and began to pray out loud.

That was it? No questions... nothing?

A few minutes later the wait staff set plates wafting with sweet and savory aromas in front of each guy.

Cameron looked at Zane from across the table. "Hey, a bunch of us are going rafting on the Snake later this morning. Want to join us?"

"Yeah, come, bro," said Tony from beside him. "I know you don't have anything better to do, and you said you wanted to get on the river one of these days. Quinn's guiding."

"It's going to be great," added Ben. "You don't want to miss it."

"Uh..." Why not? Tony was right. He didn't have any other plans besides moping around the house trying to get up the nerve to talk to Kenia. She'd be at the bookstore this morning, and that was not the place for his confessional. "Okay, sure. When and where?"

"Rafting? *This* is your brilliant idea?" Kenia stared at Alaina then pointed at her belly. "Don't you think it's a bad idea with the baby? Because I'm not going without you."

Her friend secured a ponytail in her long hair. "I'm coming. This is as safe as a carousel at the carnival. The baby will be fine."

"You couldn't have talked the twins into something as tame as a carousel."

"Too true. But Quinn says the section of river we're going on today really is safe. The boys and I will sit in the middle. Cheri's coming, too, and bringing her daughter. Harmony is even younger."

"And not such a daredevil." Kenia raised her eyebrows. "You really think the twins will stay put in the middle?"

"Their dad gave them a firm lecture."

Like that had ever made a difference before. Had Zane been that kind of kid? Bouncing from one scrape to another? Probably. "I don't know if this is a good idea."

"Since when do you play it safe? You've been moping around for two weeks. We're giving you a chance to spend time with Zane where he can't get away unless he jumps overboard and swims for it."

Kenia shuddered. "Don't even say that."

"You girls almost ready?" called Cameron from the other room. "I don't think I can keep these two contained much longer."

"I can't believe you're playing matchmaker."

Alaina threw back her head and laughed. "After what all you did when Cameron and I were dating and going through difficulties? You bet I'm interfering." She lowered her voice and nudged Kenia's shoulder. "You'll thank me later. It took a lot of phone calls to get the gang together for this."

"Everyone knows?"

"Umm... maybe?"

"Alaina!"

"I didn't have much choice. I needed to make sure I could pull it off." Her friend linked arms with her. "You look great, by the way. Time to go."

⌁

Zane snapped on the life vest Quinn handed him. The large raft, equipped to hold a dozen or more people, swayed gently in the current beside the dock.

"This is going to be fun!" Maisie announced. "Where are Evan and Oliver?"

"They'll be here any time." Ben glanced at Zane.

What was that supposed to mean? He'd already discovered this wasn't an all-guys excursion. That was okay. Cheri, the worker from the daycare, spoke with Quinn while her little daughter clung to her hand. Was something going on his housemate had forgotten to mention? Not that Zane had told Quinn much about Kenia.

"Wait for us. We're coming!" yelled a young voice.

Zane turned and looked up the walkway just as a running Evan Kraus tripped over a rock. Blood bubbled on the young boy's leg. Cameron scooped up his son and set him on the grass beside the path, while Quinn grabbed the first aid kit from the raft then jogged over.

Kenia. She was here, hurrying toward Cameron and Evan with Alaina. Zane's mouth dried. She was gorgeous in that yellow top and a pair of denim shorts that showed off her long legs. Tony was right. Zane couldn't just let her go. He might not think he had anything to offer, not with that ugly job review hanging over his head, but with his precious new glasses, maybe there really were possibilities. Opportunities.

Alaina bent over her son, but Kenia's gaze locked onto Zane's across the accident scene. Time stood still. The babble of voices faded. The riverbank, the raft, and their friends all dimmed. Only two people existed. Kenia... and Zane.

He moved toward her, feeling like the world ran in slow motion, like her eyes had a magnetic pull on his heart. Maybe they did. He stopped beside her, his arms itching to gather her close, his lips yearning for the taste of hers. "Kenia."

"Hi, Zane."

She sounded so normal. So matter-of-fact, like the past few weeks hadn't happened. No, more than that. Like the past few *months* hadn't happened. But they had.

"I'm sorry," he blurted out.

Her eyebrows rose into her orange hair. He wanted to run his fingers through it. Muss up those perfect strands a little. Hold her face in his hands. Kiss her.

But there was a guarded expression in her blue eyes. "For what?"

"For pushing you away in my pride." He wrenched his gaze away, looking down, but her legs weren't the best place for his focus, either. "I know I don't have anything to be proud of, so that was really dumb of me."

"Zane."

He flicked a glance at her, but their eyes caught again. Right, he was going to stop apologizing for things he couldn't help. Things like the debilitating syndrome that had sucked hope out of him for most of his life. It wasn't his fault. He took a deep breath. "I was mad at you because you knew things about my job I didn't know you knew. Instead, I should have been in awe that you knew, but were still willing to be seen with me."

Her gaze softened. "You're not your job, Zane. I need to apologize, too. I pushed you to consider careers with long years of college. First, it's none of my business what you do." She quirked a grin. "But, also, I don't really want you to leave Arcadia Valley for four or more years."

Zane couldn't have looked away if he tried.

"Unless you want to, of course."

He brushed a strand of hair away from her eyes. "Why not?"

Kenia's voice was barely above a whisper. "I'd miss you too much."

"Really?"

She nodded then her whole body jerked as Oliver slammed into her, breaking the moment. She pitched into Zane's arms, and he was glad to catch her.

"You screamed like a girl," Oliver taunted his twin.

"Did not."

"Eeek!" squealed Oliver, dancing away.

Evan took a swipe at him with one hand even as he rubbed his eyes with the other, smearing dirt on his damp face. "It's not even broken or anything." He almost sounded disappointed as he pointed at the neat white bandage. No doubt it would be covered in dirt in five minutes flat.

Zane chuckled as he released Kenia and let his fingers tangle with hers. They'd talk more later. Meanwhile, his heart felt lighter. A few hours on the river with sunshine and spray on their faces and adrenaline pumping through their veins would be the perfect backdrop for a perfect day.

Chapter 22

"YOU DIDN'T HAVE TO COME."

Kenia looked up at Zane. "I know, but I wanted to be here for you. Besides, I have to take advantage of Aunt Irene filling in at the store while she's still around."

Around them, the fragrance of the mock orange bushes sweetened the air in front of Retro Village. The beds lining the walkway flourished with petunias, dianthus, and pansies from the seedlings Granddad and the others had planted at Grace earlier in the spring. It was a day made for hope, but it was hard to cling to.

Zane grasped both her hands. "Whatever happens in there is okay. Really. It's not like I'm getting fired. Workers are let go all the time because of budget cuts."

She pinched back her words. They'd already been said, after all. It would be better if Zane could leave Retro on his own terms — because he had a better opportunity elsewhere — but this employment review had arrived before he'd had the chance to make any solid plans. He was still trying to get accustomed to the idea of having any options at all.

"I just wanted to be here. I'm not coming inside." Kenia pointed at the bench facing a bubbling water feature. "I'll be right there, praying for you."

Zane pressed a kiss to her forehead, sending a tremor through her body. "Thank you. So long as you know I didn't expect this of you. I will always gratefully accept your prayers." He lifted her chin. "You know I do the same for you, too, right? Every day. Many times."

"I'm so thankful." Plus, they'd prayed together every evening since the rafting trip last Saturday. A man who was growing in the Lord and desiring to be a spiritual leader? She could get on board with that.

"I don't want to keep Mr. Davis waiting." Zane's lips swept hers. "See you soon."

He strode through as the doors to the reception area slid open soundlessly. His dark hair brushed the crew neck of his white T-shirt, which hung over his faded jeans.

Kenia shook her head with a little grin. And she'd briefly thought this man should go to college to be a doctor or a lawyer? He'd hate every minute of wearing a lab coat or, worse, a suit and tie. He wasn't made for it, reading ability aside. God had planted an oak when he created Zane. Planting acorns did not result in apple trees. Nothing wrong with either of them.

She wandered over to the wrought iron bench and took a seat, lifting her face to the sunshine and closing her eyes. "Lord? Thank You for making Zane just the way he is. He's pretty amazing."

A few songbirds chirruped to each other, and a bee buzzed by. The little fountain burbled. Traffic noises droned in the distance. The flowers' sweet scent tickled her nostrils, and the warm sunshine settled over her like a tranquil blanket.

"I know You've got big plans for Zane, Lord. He has so many talents. He has such a good heart. I pray You'll reveal those plans to him, that You'll encourage him during this meeting right now."

She'd had daydreams of them sharing the apartment above the bookstore, but then she'd seen his house. He'd poured so much of himself into that renovation. He'd had great ideas, figured out how to follow through with them even without the ability to read, and taken fastidious care with the implementation. The final result spoke for itself. Too bad she couldn't hire him for the bookstore expansion, but she'd already contracted Matt Gonzalez.

Guilt poked her. She'd done that against Zane's guidance and could only hope the decision wouldn't come back to bite her.

"Kenia? What are you doing here?"

Her eyes flew open at her father's voice. "Dad? Oh,

man, you surprised me."

"You surprised me, too." He looked at her thoughtfully. "I wasn't expecting to see you here."

"I'm waiting for Zane. He's meeting with Mr. Davis right now."

Dad grimaced. "I know."

Of course, he knew. "I love him, Dad."

"I wish—"

Kenia held up her hand. "I will never find a man who loves me more. Who loves Jesus more. I know that's all you really want for me."

He shifted from one foot to the other. "Maybe a man who has employment?"

Yeah, that's about what she'd figured. "There are other jobs. He works hard. He'll find something."

Dad settled onto the bench beside Kenia. "Honey, there are things you should know about Zane. Not only did he not go to college, but he didn't even finish high school."

"I know."

Her father sent her a sharp look. "And still you date him?"

She chuckled. "It gets worse." Or, at least, it would seem like it to her parents. "He has a form of learning disability. Scotopic Sensitivity Syndrome."

"I haven't heard of it."

Education didn't teach a person everything about every subject, apparently. "He couldn't read. Not because he's stupid — trust me, he's anything but that — but because the words wouldn't hold still on the page. He was tested just a few weeks ago and fitted with a pair of glasses with colored lenses that help him focus."

Dad's eyebrows rose. "Kenia, that is such a far-fetched—"

"It's true. Search it out online. Zane's already looking into how to get his GED. He can do anything he sets his mind to. But even if he keeps his job as activities coordinator or something similar, I don't care, so long as he's happy."

Her father's mouth opened and closed.

She pushed her point. "I don't need him to support me. For that matter, the bookstore could support us both, support a family."

"You've thought all this through. You sound like you want to marry this man."

Her heart thrilled. "Yes, Dad. We've had some growing pains in our relationship, for sure. The fact we got through them proves to me that we can weather the storms so long as we stay rooted in Jesus. Deep down, I know that's what you want for me. A godly partner for life, like Joanna is for Grady. Like Mom is for you."

He sighed as he put his arm around her shoulders and tugged her close. "You're my baby girl. You're right. All I want for you is to remain strong in your faith with a good man by your side. Being healthy is great, but not always within our grasp. I guess the same is true of financial security, the way the stock market fluctuates. We've had some rough years in the garden center, too, but God has taken care of us. Blessed us."

Kenia leaned against his strong shoulder. "Thanks, Dad. Can you talk to Mom? Help her to see?"

"I can. I will. But maybe we need to make more of an effort to get to know Zane with unbiased eyes. Come to lunch on Sunday, both of you?"

"I'll check with him to see if he's made other plans, and I'll let you know."

Dad nodded. "I should get back to the garden center. I've probably left your brother to his own devices long enough."

She chuckled. "Grady's fine. You've taught him well."

"The business will be in good hands when your mother and I retire. As will Page Turners, even without your aunt." He rose to his feet. "I love you, honey."

"I love you, Dad."

Kenia watched her father stride over to his Lexus. She hadn't even noticed it when she'd pulled up beside Zane's old truck. She'd been focused on her beloved. With a lighter heart, she turned back to prayer.

"We'll be posting the position at ten hours a week

and counting on volunteers to fill in any gaps. I wish the outcome could have been different." Mr. Davis eyed Zane across the desk. "Is it too much to ask for you to consider staying on with cut hours? You've done a fine job."

"A man needs full time work, sir. I'll be looking for something else." Zane rose to his feet in the small office. At least the words *fine job* had been attributed to him. He waited as Mr. Davis stood. "Would you be willing to write a letter of recommendation?"

"I can definitely do that. Check with the front desk tomorrow morning. I'll make sure it's there."

"Thank you, sir."

"One more thing. You will be staying until the end of June, won't you? That's when the budget cuts officially take place."

The temptation rose to walk out and never look back, but the referral meant too much in such a small town. Not only that, but it was never a good idea to burn bridges, and he had a few projects to close out. "Unless I find a different job that requires me to start immediately, that's my plan."

"Okay, good. I appreciate it."

Zane reached over the desk and shook the proffered hand. Then he nodded and left the office. The receptionist gave him a sympathetic grimace as he strode through the foyer, the sliding doors parting silently at his approach.

Warm sunshine slammed into him as his gaze found Kenia, sitting on the garden bench with her eyes closed. Praying still? Or maybe asleep. He filled his mind with the image of her, her orange hair flawlessly in place, her long lashes resting on her cheeks above a perfect mouth, made for kissing. Her trim figure in a wildly patterned green top and gray capris. Toes with bright green polish poked out of orange heeled sandals.

He grinned. She was a unique flower in God's garden of humanity, never worrying what others thought of her. Just as his heart belonged to her, hers belonged to him. *Lord, thank You for the gift of this amazing woman. I want to spend my life with her, but I need a way to support her. Support the children I hope You will bless us with. Please open the doors You want me to walk through.*

A butterfly lighted on Kenia's arm, and her eyes sprang open. Then her gaze found Zane's, and she bounced to her feet. The butterfly took flight to the flowers surrounding the little fountain.

"How did it go?" She walked into his arms, and he closed them around her.

"Two weeks' notice. The budget was cut." He rested his cheek on her hair. "Just as I thought."

"I've been thinking—"

"Don't." Zane chuckled. "You've got enough to think about with the bookstore renovation. Let me worry about my own employment, okay? God will provide what I need." He slid his hands up and down her back, reveling in the feel of her body pressed against his.

"I'll try. But I'm a fixer."

"I love that about you but, this time, it's not on you. Pray. Trust God. Trust me."

She tipped her face toward his. "Okay."

He couldn't help grinning. It sounded easy, but it wouldn't be. She'd slip up a time or two, for sure. He pulled his fingers through her hair and touched his forehead to hers.

"You're messing up my hair."

"I hope I'm messing up more than that. Live a little, Kenia. Walk on the wild side."

Her face was so close that their breath mingled. Her blue eyes stared into his. "I've got a bit of a reputation for that."

"Let's be crazy together." He nearly said more, words he should wait to say, but her lips caught at his and distracted him thoroughly.

"What kind of crazy did you have in mind?" she whispered.

"A whole lot of it." Passionate crazy. Married crazy. Faces-to-the-wind crazy. He hoped his eyes made the promise his words couldn't. Not yet. Soon.

"My dad was here."

Zane blinked and pulled his head back a little. "Oh?" Even the thought of how her parents disliked him barely cooled his ardor. They'd come around... wouldn't they?

And, if not, Kenia had chosen him, anyway. He pushed aside the thought that his own parents didn't even know Kenia existed. He was going to have to get in touch, as soon as he had a job again. Then it would be up to them whether to be part of his life or not.

"He understands, Zane. At least, he's trying to."

"I'm not sure what you mean."

"I told him I love you. That I believe God has brought us together." She gave a little chuckle. "I asked him to talk to Mom and get her on the straight and narrow. He agreed... and asked if we had plans for Sunday lunch."

His eyebrows rose. "They're willing to give me a chance? He knows I'm jobless?"

Kenia grimaced. "He knows. But he trusts me enough to trust you, and he'll make sure Mom is on her best behavior."

"We can go for lunch if you want. It's up to you."

"I'd like to. I love my parents. My brother and sister-in-law. I want them to love you, too."

"Love, huh? You use that word a lot."

Her hands framed his face, rubbing gently on his stubbly cheeks, tracing his dimple. "I've told you before, and I'll tell you again. I love you, Zane Russell."

"Kenia." He swept his lips over her forehead. "I love you, too."

Chapter 23

*K*ENIA STARED AT THE HEADLINES on the Valley Times on the bookstore counter: *Local Contractor Sued for Shoddy Work.*

Her eyes caught the lead paragraph. *Matt Gonzalez, owner of Gonzalez Construction, faces charges of criminal negligence in the case of...*

She groaned. It couldn't be.

Zane's arms came around her from behind. "I'm sorry, sweetheart. I take it you hadn't heard."

She shook her head as she twisted to face him. "I can't believe it. It's the third week in July. Matt's supposed to start here next week. I've got calluses on my hands from breaking down walls and shoveling debris into the dumpster." Not that Zane hadn't helped when he could. She could hear her voice rising. "It's not like I can rent out the other half to anyone else in the condition it is now, and it could be a year before another contractor is free to pick up the job." Think of all the money tied up in that empty space.

"It'll be okay." Zane rubbed her back.

Kenia pulled away. "Easy for you to say."

His hands dropped by his sides as he tilted his head. "Not really. It hurts me to see you hurting."

She needed to stop thinking like a loner. It wasn't all about her. Sure, she'd always been surrounded by friends and family but still walked to the beat of her own drums. Zane was part of her life now. Hopefully a permanent part. She massaged her temples. "I'm sorry. Next you're going to tell me that this was no surprise to God."

A grin quirked one side of Zane's mouth and a twinkle lit his eyes. "Sounds like I don't need to tell you what you already know."

"It's just—" Kenia wadded up the paper and threw it as hard as she could. It hit a spinner rack and floated to the floor like a feather. Totally unsatisfactory. She growled. "I wish there was still something next door to smash."

Zane tipped his head back and let out a deep guffaw. "That's my girl."

She glared at him, but the flash of anger was already dissipating. "What am I going to do?"

"First, we — not just you — are going to pray."

"Yeah. Good plan."

"And then we're going to see what God does."

"I don't suppose *you* could..."

"Take over the job?" Zane shook his head. "I don't have the business ability or the connections. Besides, working for Harrison Renovation is taking fifty hours a week as it is."

She sighed. "And Drew is too busy. I know." If only she'd fired Matt when he'd quit returning her calls back in June. Maybe she could have convinced Zane then, before he'd started working for Drew. But, no. He hadn't been qualified to take on commercial work then, either. "I stink at making business decisions."

Zane lifted her chin. "That is not true. No negative self-talk, remember?"

He'd learned well. Too bad she hadn't.

"It's called faith for a reason, sweetheart. It will all work out. You'll see."

"I've got so many people counting on a retail outlet for their work since I put the word out. Serena with her pottery. Allie with the lavender. Riley Taylor called a few days ago to see if she could display some of her dog paintings. There've been other inquiries."

Zane quirked a grin. "It will all work out. I need to have something to spend that gift certificate on."

Kenia shook her head. "It's not funny. What do I tell them?"

Seven days wasn't enough time for a miracle. Her conscience jabbed. God didn't operate on her timeline. He never had, and He wouldn't start this week, just because she was panicking. She needed to breathe. To trust. To be thankful she wasn't the one with collapsing walls suing Gonzalez Construction. Kenia took a long, shuddering breath.

His arms wrapped around her. "They'll know it's not your fault. And, they're women of faith. They'll pray with you."

She might feel the sensations of safety in his strong arms, but God's arms were infinitely stronger. She was secure. Cared for. Cherished by her heavenly Father.

"And so will I." He did just that, out loud, in the middle of Page Turners.

Zane heard footsteps on the back staircase. "Shhh! Everyone ready?"

The apartment's living room was jam-packed full of people. Not just any people. Kenia's family. Their friends.

"I'm exhausted," he heard Kenia say then the key clicked in the lock. "Thanks for helping me clean the cot—"

"Happy birthday!" everyone shouted.

She screamed, her eyes wide, then her hand clamped over her mouth and her gaze arrowed straight at Zane. "You didn't."

"Guilty." He laughed and closed the gap before

taking her in his arms and kissing her, right in front of everyone.

"But I..." Kenia looked around.

She must've realized that the packing boxes had disappeared. Zane had seen to stacking them carefully in the two spare bedrooms and making sure all the living room furniture was in place along with a raft of folding chairs he'd borrowed from Grace Fellowship. Her fridge, empty of food on moving day, had been loaded with gallons of iced tea and large bowls of salad, to say nothing of a giant box of donuts Jonah had dropped by earlier.

Kenia whirled and collided with Evelyn, who stood behind her. "Did you know? Of course you knew."

Maisie edged past the two women, wearing a proud smirk. "We all knew, and we didn't tell. Zane, can we eat? I'm starving. Kenia worked me *so hard*, washing out all the cupboards in the cottage."

"Eat?" Kenia turned back to him.

At the bottom of the stairs, the doorbell rang. Zane grinned. "I'll just go get that, okay? Can I get some help?"

Tony and Ben nodded and followed him down. He'd already paid for the delivery from Fire and Brimstone. Now they carried stacks of pizza boxes up to the buzzing apartment. They spread them open on the long folding table while others set out the salads and drinks.

Zane stuck his fingers in his mouth and let out a shrill

whistle. The large room instantly quieted. "Let's get this party started, shall we? Let me say grace." He slipped his arm around Kenia's waist and closed his eyes. "Lord, we are so thankful for all the blessings You provide in our lives. I want to thank You for Kenia. Thank You for blessing the Akers family with her twenty-nine years ago today."

Kenia jabbed his ribs.

He grinned, but kept his eyes shut. "Thank You for Page Turners. We ask that You will bless this bookstore. Thank You for friends who make our lives complete and walk with us through life. Please bless this food and bless our time together this evening. In Jesus' name, amen."

A chorus of voices echoed the amen.

Zane turned Kenia to the table and handed her a plate.

Her eyebrows rose. "Paper?"

"Did you have a fifty-place setting of dishes tucked away somewhere that I didn't know about?"

She laughed. "Not so much. These pizzas smell amazing. I don't even know which to try first."

"That one and that one." Maisie pointed. "Can I go next? I'm so weak I'm going to pass out any minute."

"Right behind the birthday girl," Zane promised. "If she'll ever get started."

What a perfect evening.

Kenia sat on a chair in front of the window and couldn't stop beaming at so many friends gathered in one place. Ben and Evelyn had helped Zane set the whole thing up. Of course, Alaina and Cameron were here, with Maisie riding herd on the twins on the floor in the corner while Harmony giggled at their antics, and Cheri watched over them all. Serena and Micah had come, and even Ursula and Malachi, though they stayed off to one side while Ursula signed rapidly to Mal. Tony and Quinn were here. Allie and Cole, who'd pulled off a surprise wedding back in June, chatted with Veronica and her new boyfriend, Lucas. Drew and Kate had even come, probably because Zane was working for Harrison Renovations.

And her family, too. Grady strutted like a peacock, while Joanna's belly cleared her path around the room. Mom and Aunt Irene chatted in the kitchen, and Dad had Micah cornered with a deep-sounding business conversation.

Sitting beside her, Zane squeezed her hand. "Happy?"

"I can't believe you pulled this off. It's perfect."

He leaned a little closer and spoke softly. "Perfect?" Those brown eyes darkened, and the fire she loved so much smoldered in their depths. His breath warmed her cheek. "Can you think of any way it could be even better? You've handed in the keys to the cottage, moved into your new apartment, and taken over the reins of a successful business. You're surrounded by people who love you. What could be better?"

She looked into his precious face. Did she dare just come out and say it? Why not? She'd always gone after what she wanted before. So far, it had all worked out... other than the renovation still on hold downstairs. "You," she whispered. "You could make it better."

"Like this?" Without breaking his gaze, he turned and slid to one knee on the floor in front of her.

Her hands flew to cover her mouth. Was he really...? Right here, in front of everyone? Right now? She'd only been kidding. Sort of.

Zane dug into his pocket and came up with a small velvet box. *Facets on Main* was written in gold filigree on the burgundy box.

He was.

Kenia jiggled in her seat and squealed. She couldn't help it. Her gaze bounced between Zane's grinning face and the sparkle of the diamond he slowly revealed.

"Kenia, I love you. Will you—"

"Yes!" She threw her arms around his neck, nearly toppling him backward. "Yes, I will."

Maybe the room had gone silent. She couldn't tell for sure. Didn't care.

"You didn't let me finish." Zane gave her an aggrieved look. "I have an entire speech."

She jammed her hands under her thighs and tried to

sit still. "Okay. Sorry. Go ahead." She schooled her expression.

"I was just going to ask you if you wanted to go rafting on the Snake one of these evenings."

Kenia glared at him. "You are such a brat."

"I can totally hook you up with a moonlight float if you want," hollered Quinn.

She ducked her chin and raised her eyebrows at Zane.

He rocked back with laughter then sobered. "Kenia, will you marry me?"

Kenia tapped her chin. "Well, now, I don't know for sure. A guy who plays tricks like that with my heart — I'm not sure he can be trusted."

"Maybe I can bribe you with this." He tipped the little box toward her. "Maybe I can bribe you with promises of forever."

She touched her fingertip to the gleaming diamond. "You might have talked me into it. I love you, Zane."

He tugged the understated but gorgeous ring from its nest and slipped it on her finger.

"It's a perfect fit." She fluttered her hand, loving the feel of the ring and how it caught the light. Thrilled by what it represented.

Zane chuckled. "Facets has your ring size on record. Come here." He pulled her to standing and wrapped both arms around her so tightly she could barely breathe. His face burrowed into the crook of her neck as she held him just as snugly. "I love you, Kenia. Thank you."

"Kiss me," she whispered.

His mouth covered hers, tasting and giving and promising a lifetime of love.

"Eww, don't look," came Evan's voice.

Applause and whistling cat-calls filled the apartment as Kenia leaned back in the arms of her beloved and gazed into his precious eyes.

"I've got a birthday gift for you," he said.

"You've already—"

"No, there's more." Zane loosened his hold and turned to stand beside her, one arm firmly around her waist.

"I guess that's my cue." Drew rose and crossed the crowded room. "Kenia, I was really sorry to hear about Matt Gonzalez last week. He left a lot of people in the lurch, including you. Kate and I prayed about what we could do, and God answered our prayer."

Kenia glanced up at Zane, but he was focused on his boss.

"Harrison Renovation has expanded. I've been able to hire the best of Matt's crew, and you probably realize that Zane here is pretty talented himself."

She definitely knew that. She'd seen his house. Her breath held.

"So, we have enough work for two crews and, now, enough men to do it. I'm putting Zane in charge of one of the teams. I'll need him to complete a job for Bigby Farms through August, but he and his crew can start with the Page Turners expansion by mid-September. Does that work for you?"

Kenia blinked back tears. "It sure does. I'd hoped to be open and running by Thanksgiving."

"Barring unforeseen circumstances, that shouldn't be a problem. You won't need to close during construction, except for a few days when we break through the wall. It'll get kind of messy then. Zane and I will keep you abreast of progress."

"That totally works for me." She clasped her hands together. "I can't believe it. I thought all hope was gone until next year."

Zane nuzzled her hair. "Believe it... and happy birthday."

"Oh, it is." She threw her arms around Drew, rocking him backward. "Thank you."

He laughed and patted her shoulders. "You're welcome. I'm glad to help."

"Happy birthday, honey." Dad stepped in for a hug. "You've got a good man there. Your mother and I are honored to have him join the family."

Kenia glanced at Zane, who was accepting back slaps from his buddies. "He is something special, for sure. Thanks, Dad."

Mom wrapped her arms around Kenia. "Congratulations, sweetheart. May I see your ring?"

Kenia lifted her hand, admiring the sparkle once again. She almost missed the quick glance between her parents and the slight warning look on Dad's face.

"That's lovely." Mom pursed her lips.

"It's not the size of the diamond that matters, Mom. It's the size of the love. And Zane has that in abundance."

"That's so true." Her mother smiled. "You are a wise woman."

Dear Reader

Do you share my passion for locally grown real food? No, I'm not as fanatical or fixated as many of the characters I write about, but gardening, cooking, and food processing comprise a large part of my non-writing life.

Whether you're new to the concept or a long-time advocate, I invite you to my website and blog at www.valeriecomer.com to explore God's thoughts on the junction of food and faith.

Please sign up for my monthly newsletter while you're there! My thank-you gift to all subscribers is *Promise of Peppermint*, a prequel to the Urban Farm Fresh Romance series. Joining my list is the best way to keep tabs on my food/farm life as well as contests, cover reveals, deals, and news about upcoming books. I welcome you!

Enjoy this Book?

Please leave a review at any online retailer or reader site. Letting other readers know what you think about *Harvest of Love: An Arcadia Valley Romance* helps them make a decision and means a lot to me. Thank you!

If you haven't read any of my other books, may I suggest the six-book Farm Fresh Romances? The first story is *Raspberries and Vinegar*.

Keep reading for the first chapter of *The Taste of Romance* by Danica Favorite, the next book in the multi-author Arcadia Valley Romance series.

The Taste

of Romance

— an Arcadia Valley Romance —

DANICA FAVORITE

Chapter One

S O THIS WAS BIGBY FARM. Madison McKay pulled into the driveway and took in the buildings around her. To her left was a sprawling yellow farmhouse with random-looking, tacked on bits that must have been added over the years. Straight ahead were a series of barns and a large parking lot. And to the right was a large field of narrow, purple flowers that looked like lavender. Though they'd passed many farms along the way that reeked of manure, this place smelled fresh, clean. A far cry from the ramshackle dump her mother used to complain about. Actually, to hear her mother speak of Bigby farm, one would think it was one of the levels of hell as described in Dante's Inferno. Which ring depended upon how charitable her mother was feeling toward her in-laws.

275

Madison didn't have very many memories of the Bigby side of the family. Her dad had died when she was young, and her mother had cut off all contact, blaming the Bigbys for her husband's death and saying they would ruin Madison's life. They hadn't. Madison had done a fine job of ruining her life all on her own. Which was why she found herself walking up the steps of the front porch with her three children. D.J., Faith, and two-year-old Hope, the bonus baby everyone thought would make things better, but had marked the beginning of the end for the marriage. Not that it was Hope's fault. In many ways, Madison was grateful for the tiny little girl who'd given her the strength to do the right thing when she had lost her ability to see straight.

Which is why it didn't seem so crazy that she'd accepted a long-lost cousin's invitation to stay with their grandmother while she figured out how to get back on her feet after her husband ran off to an ashram in India with his yoga instructor. The kind of thing she thought only happened in movies, but now, it was real life. The problem with spending her entire adult life as a stay-at-home mom was that when her husband took all the money, leaving her with nothing but debt and three children who didn't stop growing simply because she couldn't afford to buy them new clothes, she didn't have a lot of options.

She knocked on the front door, but was met with silence. She'd told them to expect her around four, and it was five until. Maybe they were running late, and she was just a tad bit early.

"What is this place?" D. J. asked, looking around. "Is this where Dad is?"

Every single day. She had to answer the exact same question. Where was their father? Neither she nor the kids had heard from him in nearly six months. It must have felt even longer to the kids, who didn't understand why their father was on a quest to find himself. David McKay, a solid member of the community, active in his kids' lives, and from the outside, the picture-perfect example of what a father should be. At least until the morning he didn't return from his business trip, and instead sent her an email, telling her he needed time to figure out who he was.

As many times as she'd read that email, and the few that had come since, Madison still didn't understand. So how could she get her children to?

"No. I told you. We're going to stay with my grandmother and my cousins for a while. Won't it be fun to have family around us?"

One more thing the children had no concept of. Both Madison and Dave had been only children, and Dave's parents were long gone. Madison's mother was also an only child, and the lack of connection to the Bigbys, until now, had meant that they didn't have many family connections. When they'd gotten together, Madison and Dave had planned on having a large family. D.J.'s early arrival and rushed wedding was supposed to be the start of their dreams coming true. But after Faith, Dave's career took off, and he thought everything was just perfect. All the people he tried to impress had a similarly perfect family with a son, a daughter, and a trophy wife. Little did those perfect people know, all it took to fall from the pedestal was another unplanned pregnancy and subsequent weight gain that was a lot harder to bounce back from at thirty than it had been at twenty. At least, that's what Madison assumed had been the problem, based on all Dave's fat jokes.

The kids hadn't answered Madison's question, but she hadn't expected them to. They wore the same shell-shocked expression that hadn't left their faces since she'd told them their father wasn't coming home. How could it make sense to them, when everything had seemed fine prior to Dave's leaving? It wasn't until the bill collectors started calling and Madison started digging into their finances that she realized her husband had been leading a double life for years.

Fabulous for Dave, that he could find a way to start all over in creating his dream life. And goody for him that after years of feeling like he'd lost himself, he could now find the path to enlightenment. She just wished he'd had the guts to explain it to his kids.

She took Hope's hand. "Why don't we walk around and take a look at the farm while we wait?"

"Maybe we can find a place with Wi-Fi," D.J. said,

the usual irritation lining his voice.

She'd had to give up their cell plan a few months ago, when the money had run out. No, not money. Their credit limit. What had Dave been thinking, buying the kids expensive cell phones just before he left and not leaving Madison a way to pay for it? Everyone thought she just haven't tried hard enough or was sitting around, doing nothing all day. But she had literally never held a job. As a teenager, her mother hadn't let her work, wanting her to focus on her studies. The same for college. Since she'd left school a semester before graduation to have D. J., she'd been a stay-at-home mom. When she'd talked about going back to school and finishing her degree or even finding a job, so she could do something with herself while the kids were in school, Dave would get angry and asked her why the life he'd given her wasn't enough.

Though she'd never been one for violence, sometimes she wanted to punch him in the nose for that one. He'd left her completely alone with no options for survival because his life wasn't enough, but she was supposed to have been satisfied with the way he had left her helpless.

"I'm hungry," Faith said.

They'd passed a fast food place about an hour ago, and even though the kids begged to stop, Madison had pressed on, eager to get here, but also painfully aware that she had less than $100 to her name and she wasn't sure how long she would need it to stretch. She'd been ashamed to explain her financial situation to her grandmother and cousin Allie. Especially since her mother said she'd brought it on herself. Her mother was another person who didn't understand why Dave had left. The perfect husband didn't suddenly decide he hated his life, so surely Madison had done something wrong.

Well, she could admit to a lot of things, but mostly she'd been wrong in blindly trusting him and thinking they were happy. She'd thought that that's what you're supposed to do in a marriage, and had Dave given her any indication that he wanted things to be different, she would have done her best to change. But other than going on more diets to combat his snide comments about her weight, and visiting a counselor he refused to see, she hadn't known what else to do.

Fortunately, before Madison could patiently explain once again that they still had some carrots to snack on in the car, a man came around the side of the house.

All three children huddled closer to her, and as Madison looked at the man, she couldn't help putting her arms around them. If they weren't on the farm in the middle of nowhere, she would have thought he was one of those homeless men you saw on streets, begging for food. His hair was long and shaggy, and his beard wasn't the neatly kept hipster style of the men they knew back home, even though he couldn't have been much older than them. He wore baggy, dirty jeans, and a T-shirt that looked like it belonged in the rag pile as opposed to on a man's body. His hands and arms were covered in dirt all the way up to his elbows. Mud caked his clothing.

"If you're here to sell Enid something, she's not interested. Nice touch bringing the kids though." Then he paused. "It's not cookie season, is it? School's out for the year, but…"

She opened her mouth to explain who she was, but didn't get the chance.

He looked them up and down. "Oh, wait. I forgot the youth group is doing a fundraiser for camp. I'm sorry. I should have guessed that with you bringing the kids, that was the case. You must be the new family to town. Sorry we haven't had a chance to meet, but I've been gone the past couple of weeks."

"Wade Ellis." He held out his filthy hand.

Madison must've given him a funny look, because he looked down at it, then groaned.

"Sorry about that," he said, brushing his hand on his equally filthy pants. "I've been transplanting lavender for Allie all day, and I didn't pay much attention to my appearance coming out to see who was on Enid's front porch."

At least now, things were starting to make sense. Her cousin Allie used Bigby farm to run a lavender operation. She grew lavender and made all kinds of products out of it that she sold at various farmers markets and regional boutiques. This man must be a migrant worker she hired during her busy season.

"I hope I didn't offend you too much with my comments about you guys trying to sell us something. A lot of people want to take advantage of an old woman living alone, and I get a little protective. Still, I'm always happy to support the youth group." He reached into his back pocket and pulled out a wallet. "What fundraiser did they decide on? None of the other kids have hit me up yet, but I'm always happy to donate to everyone."

Was it weird to like someone so immediately? The guy might be a migrant worker, but to be willing to donate to every kid going to camp was pretty special. He reminded her of Mrs. Sanders, who lived down the block from her growing up. Even though the old widow had no money, any time any of the kids came by with the school fundraiser, she always pressed a quarter into their hands, telling them it wasn't much, but she hoped it would help. People like this Wade guy and Mrs. Sanders always made her feel ashamed for how she and Dave used to live. They'd had plenty of money, and while they gave their requisite tithes to the church, it certainly wasn't the kind of sacrificial giving she saw here.

She smiled at him. "Thank you, but we're not here for a donation. I'm Madison McKay, Enid's granddaughter, and we're here for a visit."

Wade's eyes widened. "Allie said you weren't coming until the fifth."

"Today is the fifth." She tried not to sound rude in her answer, especially because this guy was trying to be helpful.

He shook his head, looking disgusted. "I'm so sorry. I should pay better attention to the calendar. Allie is going to kill me when she finds out." Then he grinned. "But she'll get over it as soon as she meets you. I don't know who was more excited, Allie or Enid. I guess I don't need to tell you how much Allie has enjoyed emailing with you."

This man sounded much more familiar with the family's inner workings than a seasonal migrant worker. But as Madison mentally went through the list of family members she remembered Allie discussing with her, she couldn't recall hearing about a Wade.

"I'm looking forward to it," Madison said. "We're just waiting for them to get home."

Wade laughed. "Oh, they're home, all right. Enid was baking up a storm this morning. I'm sure they're in the kitchen waiting for you. No one uses the front door, which is why I thought you were a salesperson. Come on. Let's go say hi to everyone."

It would have been nice for Allie to warn her that no one used the front door, but as they walked around the back of the house, and she saw all the cars parked there, it would have been clear to Madison that's where she should have gone.

Before they got halfway down the walk, the door opened, and an older woman, with white hair and sparkling eyes, came rushing out. Though she looked far too young to be in her eighties, Madison knew that this was her grandmother.

A strange sense of peace filled her as Enid wrapped her arms around Madison, and the older woman whispered, "Thank you God, for answering my prayers."

Madison had gone to church her whole life, and she had never experienced such a genuine confession of gratitude as she did now. Funny, considering she saw Enid as an answer to her prayers, rather than the other way around. And yet, as she remembered Wade's words about people wanting to take advantage of an older woman, she felt slightly guilty. Though it was true Enid was offering her a place to stay to get back on her feet, Madison was also grateful to reconnect with the side of the family she didn't know. Hopefully, no one would think that the only reason she was here was for money.

She squeezed her grandmother tight. "And thank you for being an answer to mine."

Enid pulled away. "None of that. We're family. This is what family is for. Now let me meet those great-grandchildren of mine. Since everyone else around here is being stubborn about giving me some, at least now I have some youngsters to enjoy."

Madison nudged her son. "This is David Junior, but we all called him D.J. He's eleven, and he loves computer games."

She had to sell his game console a couple of months ago to help pay the electric bill. He still hadn't forgiven her, but she'd already sold everything else of value she had. At least that was one thing Dave had done right. Every holiday, he'd given her some expensive piece of jewelry or some other useless bauble that she hadn't much liked, but she'd dutifully accepted. Those had been easy to sell off. Her final act of desperation to get here had been hiring an estate sale company to liquidate everything else they had in her home, which hadn't been much since there weren't many valuables left. Now, all they had left was what she'd been able to fit in her car.

"Those things will rot your brain," her grandmother said.

D.J. scowled. "You don't know anything. My dad says I'm going to be a computer programmer someday and make a gazillion dollars."

Would Dave have left it he'd known just how much his son looked up to him?

Ignoring the temptation to argue with her son, Madison nudged Faith. "This is Faith. She's nine, and she loves animals. I think it's going to be great for her, living on a farm, where she can interact with them."

"My dad says farm animals are dirty and carry

disease," Faith said, looking smugly at her brother. Before Dave left, Faith had always argued with her father on this point. But now, the kids seemed to desperately cling to everything he'd ever said as if they thought it would somehow bring him back.

If only.

It wasn't that Madison wanted Dave back. Honestly, after everything he'd put her through, leaving her alone to figure out how to take care of her family while he found himself, she wasn't sure how she would ever be able to trust him again. Besides, the yoga instructor wasn't the first affair. It was just the first she'd found out about until she'd started going through his records.

Wade stepped forward. "They definitely can, which is why we take a lot of precautions for cleanliness here. Once you get settled in, I'll be happy to demonstrate."

Was he joking? Caked in dirt, the man was hardly the poster child for hygiene.

"You don't look like you've had a bath in months," Faith said. "How do I know we're not going to get a disease from you?"

She hadn't raised her children to speak to adults like that and it made her heart hurt to see the disgust on her daughter's face.

"Faith! That was rude. Apologize to this nice man right now. He's just trying to help."

"Our father said homeless people are a scourge on the earth and deserve everything they get," Faith continued, ignoring Madison's request completely. "Maybe, if they made better choices, they would have better lives."

She had never been ashamed of her children before. But the smug expressions on their faces made Madison want to cry. She'd had enough of protecting the man who'd turned such sweet human beings into monsters.

"Then take a look in the mirror," Madison said. "Because technically, you're homeless. So you get back to me on how to make better choices for your own life."

Tears filled Faith's eyes, and Madison regretted her harsh words. D.J., however, turned and glared at Madison. "You were the one who made bad choices. You made our dad leave. And maybe if you weren't lazy and got a job, we would still have all our stuff."

Dozens of people had said the same thing to Madison, including her own mother. Which was why Madison was here, dependent on the kindness of relatives she'd never even met. Everyone thought that Madison had to have done something wrong to have made her husband leave the way he did. No one understood why she didn't just get a job that miraculously made everything all better. But given that they'd gone from Dave's six-figure salary to nothing and the best Madison was qualified for was flipping burgers at a local fast food place that barely paid above minimum wage, it wasn't even enough to pay the utility bill. Not that they would hire her. She'd tried.

Wade took a step toward D.J. "That's enough, young man. I might look like a homeless person to you, but I would never speak to my mother like that. I don't know you folks, and I don't know where your dad is. But if I were your dad, I'd have a good talking to you about treating people with respect. Your mother's done a good thing by bringing you here. The Bigbys are the finest people I've ever known, and I hope that a little time with them will teach you about common decency."

For a moment, everyone was silent. Madison struggled with the emotions welling up inside her. She hadn't once cried in front of her children. Not even when the man from the bank came and started taking pictures of their house to sell it out from under them. It's what happened when your husband stopped paying the mortgage months before leaving and didn't tell you. But she supposed her son was right. She'd made a bad choice in trusting that Dave was taking care of everything the way he'd said he would.

Enid cleared her throat. "It's all right, Wade. I'm sure the boy didn't mean it. It's got to be hard, losing everything the way they did, and children don't understand the ways of adults."

Tears filled the older woman's eyes, threatening to break the dam holding back the emotions Madison had been stuffing down for months. She bent and picked up Hope.

"All right then, moving on." Madison pasted a smile

on her face as she gave her little girl a squeeze. "This is Hope. She's two, and an absolute delight."

"No, she's not," Faith said. "She still wets the bed."

To nine-year-olds, a bed-wetter was a terrible thing. But they had struggled with potty training, and with all the uncertainty over the past few months, it seemed more difficult than ever.

Enid held out her arms. "That's all right. I've known a number of bed-wetters in my time, and I know she'll outgrow it. I've got tea that will help."

Madison had no idea how tea would help with bed-wetting, but at this point, she was willing to give it a try.

"Now that we've met everyone," Enid said. "Let's go inside and have a snack. I'm sure you're all starving after your trip."

The kids perked up at the idea of food. Wade had said Enid had been baking all day. Maybe a few tasty treats would have them warming up to the situation.

When they got into the kitchen, the spread laid out before them made Madison's heart sink. One platter had an array of fresh vegetables, including the carrots her children were starting to dread. They were an inexpensive snack, so Madison often used them to fill hungry bellies between meals. Another platter was filled with various fruits, that Madison suspected also came from the farm. She remembered her cousin telling her about how they preferred to use local and in season produce and grew much of their own food. Before their lives had been turned upside down, Madison prided herself on preparing only local and organic meals for her children. But as she saw the expressions on her children's faces, she realized that the children were not as impressed.

At least Enid held out a tray of freshly baked cookies to the children. They'd had to give up sweets because they'd been too expensive. The children eagerly took a bite of their cookies. Then promptly spit them out.

"Gross! What's in this?" D.J. said, making a face and sticking out his tongue.

Faith glared at Madison. "This tastes like the time you put salt instead of sugar in our muffins."

She'd only done it once, right after Dave had left, and she'd been baking to try to make herself feel better. Except when you're using the baby's nap time while the kids were at school to do so, sometimes you find yourself sobbing too hard to read the recipe properly. It was the only opportunity Madison had to cry. But children didn't understand that.

"We don't use sugar here," a woman's voice said. Madison looked up and saw her cousin Allie entering the room. "I'm sorry I wasn't here to greet you, but I had a conference call with a boutique chain interested in carrying my products and it went a little long."

Allie gave her a warm hug, and Madison was once again comforted with the feeling that she'd come home. Maybe she had made a lot of really bad decisions, but they'd all brought her here, to this place, and this moment, where she finally felt like maybe everything was going to be all right.

The Taste of Romance

is available through online retailers.
Find out more at
ArcadiaValleyRomance.co

Author Biography

Valerie Comer lives where food meets faith in her real life, her fiction, and on her blog and website. She and her husband of over 35 years farm, garden, and keep bees on a small farm in Western Canada, where they grow and preserve much of their own food.

Valerie has always been interested in real food from scratch, but her conviction has increased dramatically since God blessed her with four delightful granddaughters. In this world of rampant disease and pollution, she is compelled to do what she can to make these little girls' lives the best she can. She helps supply healthy food — local food, organic food, seasonal food — to grow strong bodies and minds.

Valerie is a *USA Today* bestselling author and a two-time Word Award winner. She writes engaging characters, strong communities, and deep faith into her green clean romances.

To find out more, visit her website at www.valeriecomer.com, where you can read her blog, explore her many links, and sign up for her email newsletter. Her thank-you gift is a download of *Promise of Peppermint*, the prequel novella to the Urban Farm Fresh Romance series. You can also use this QR code to access the newsletter sign-up.